Lock Down Publications and Ca$h
Presents

I0664152

MONEY HUNGRY DEMONS 3

THERE'S NO ANGELS IN HELL

A Novel By
TRANAY ADAMS

First Edition 2024

Printed in the United States of America

Lock Down Publications
P.O. Box 944
Stockbridge, GA 30281
www.lockdownpublications.com

Like our page on Facebook: Lock Down Publications
www.facebook.com/lockdownpublications.ldp

Stay Connected with Us!

Text **LOCKDOWN** to 22828 to stay up-to-date with new releases, sneak peaks, contests and more...

Like our page on Facebook:
Lock Down Publications

Join Lock Down Publications/The New Era Reading Group

Visit our website:
www.lockdownpublications.com

Follow us on Instagram:
Lock Down Publications

Email Us: We want to hear from you!

PROLOGUE

How That Nigga Heavy Ended Up In Prison

Lump never liked the cold, but the New York winter was more than a chill, it was a full-on slap in the face. Draped in his leather jacket, he leaned against the hood of his rented Cadillac, watching from across the street. His breath came out in thick, misty puffs. He felt the tracker vibrating in his pocket, its signal steady and clear. Autumn was here. His heartbeat drummed in his ears. Every muscle in his body was tense. He didn't want to believe it, but he had to see it himself.

***

A few years earlier…

Rolo was in rare form, king of the night, swaggering like he owned the city and shit. The music boomed as he danced with a caramel-skinned joint, her laugh infectious, her hazel eyes glued to him. A Sensodyne white smile spread across Rolo's face. The man was wealthy beyond imagination, draped in a mink coat, with diamonds dancing on his neck and wrists, and he felt untouchable.

But Lump saw everything. He'd been in New York long enough to know that when a man like Rolo was feeling himself a little too much, trouble was never far behind. Sure enough, two Dominican stickup kids lurking near the bar eyed Rolo, like lions stalking a gazelle. Their hands twitched, their eyes hungry. Lump knew what was about to go down before it even happened.

He watched as Rolo left the club, dismissing his bodyguards with a wave, the girl hanging on his arm. The stickup kids made their move, guns drawn, faces tight with determination. They cornered Rolo against his car and forced him to hand over everything: the Richard Mille, the diamond earrings, the cash, even the jewelry on the woman. But Lump wasn't going to let this play out. He saw his chance and took it.

With the speed of a leopard, Lump crossed the street, his gun already out.

Bop. Bop. Bop. Bop.

The shots came clean and quick. Both stickup kids dropped before they knew what hit them. Rolo's eyes widened in shock, then gratitude.

"Good lookin' out, fam," Rolo stammered, still catching his breath. "Yo, son, you better haul ass. Nine will be in here inna minute."

Lump nodded understandingly. He went to take off, but Rolo called him back and they exchanged contact info. Once Lump had gotten ghost, Rolo cooked up a story to tell the police. Seeing their flashing red and blue lights, he waved them down and motioned them over to him.

***

The next morning, $100,000 in cash showed up at Lump's doorstep, but Lump sent it back. He wanted more than money. He wanted an opportunity, a sit-down with the man himself. He knew Rolo was a major player, the one who could give him access to the big leagues.

***

5

Rolo and Lump met, hit it off, and the business relationship flourished. Lump became his new buyer, and everything was perfect, almost too perfect.

Then, Lump noticed the way Rolo looked at Autumn. The glances that lingered a second too long, the compliments that seemed too eager, the chuckles that sounded like they held hidden meanings. And then, there was Autumn, his wife, his ride-or-die since third grade. She had a way of brushing it all off, but the tension in the air was thick enough to choke on.

Lump knew something was off. His instincts had never lied to him before, and they weren't starting now.

***

Now, here he was, waiting and watching. The front doors of the hotel opened, and his heart stopped. He saw Autumn step out of her car, her hair shining under the streetlights, her heels clicking against the concrete, looking every bit the goddess, he knew she was. He swallowed hard, hoping, praying, she was here for a friend or some innocent reason.

But then came the Maybach. Rolo stepped out; a grin spread across his face the moment he saw her. Lump's breath hitched. It was like watching a car crash in slow motion. He couldn't turn away. Rolo walked up to Autumn, wrapped his arms around her waist, and kissed her like she was his bitch. Lump's stomach twisted into knots. He felt like throwing up.

He watched, silent, cold, as his wife, his woman, entered the hotel, hand in hand with Rolo, laughing like they shared some secret joke.

Lump's vision blurred with anger and his knuckles crackled as he clenched the steering wheel. His eyes stung hot with tears, but he wasn't going to cry, not here and not now. He was past that.

His thoughts raced, and every scenario in his head ended the same way, with him putting a bullet in Rolo's wig. But he knew he couldn't just go off like that, at least not yet. He had to be smart. He had to play this hand right. He had come too far, and there was too much at stake.

He took a deep breath, steadying himself. He couldn't let emotion fuck with his judgment, not now. He needed a plan, a way to make them both pay. Because one thing was clear, he wasn't going to take a loss, not to some slick-talking kingpin or a cheating wife.

When Autumn returned home from her date with Rolo, she found Lump lounging on the couch. The living room was thick with smoke from a half-burned blunt, smoldering in the ashtray, and the air charged with tension. Two suitcases, stuffed with her clothes and personal things, stood like security guards by the door.

Lump smiled at her, but it wasn't a friendly smile. It was the kind that made her skin prickle. "Hey, baby," he said casually, "did you have fun?"

Autumn froze, a chill creeping down her spine. She knew something was off, but she couldn't quite place it. She took a second, masking her unease with a smile of her own. "Yeah, I had a great time, but I'm tired," she replied. "You know how my girls are. I was ready to come home, but they begged me to stay for MiMi's birthday." Her eyes flicked nervously to the packed bags. "You got your luggage packed. Where you going, babe?"

Lump chuckled, standing up slowly, like a lion rising to his feet. "Where I'm goin'? Nah, sweetheart, the question is, where the fuck you goin'?"

Autumn's heart skipped a beat. "What do you mean?" she asked confused.

"Don't play dumb with me, bitch," Lump growled, his smile vanishing. He whipped out his cellphone and shoved it in her face, showing her the footage of her and Rolo at the hotel, their hands all over each other. Autumn turned as pale as a ghost as she stared at the undeniable proof of her infidelity.

Without another word, Lump grabbed the suitcases and yanked them toward the door. Autumn dropped to her knees as tears flooded her cheeks. "Please, Lump, I'm sorry. I love you. I was lonely, and you were never home," she sobbed, her voice raw with desperation. She clung to his leg, her sobs guttural and unrestrained. "Please don't throw me out."

He sneered down at her. "I ain't never home 'cause I'm out here chasin' a bag to keep you in alla that expensive ass bullshit you want," he hissed. "And this is how you repay me?"

Autumn's face crumpled. "I'll do anything," she begged. "Please, just don't leave me. I'll commit suicide. I'll slit my wrists, if you leave me."

Lump's gaze was cold, unforgiving. "Bitch, you think I give a fuck? Tell that shit to Jesus, when you see 'em," he said, kicking her hand away.

But she clung tighter, her nails digging into his skin, her body trembling with fear.

"Anything?" he asked, his voice softening with a twisted curiosity.

Autumn nodded frantically, wiping her tears. "Yes, anything. Just please, don't leave me."

A slow, cruel smile spread across his lips. "Alright then, let's see how far you're willing to go."

***

For weeks, he made her crawl on her hands and knees like a dog. He had her butt naked, wearing nothing but a spiked dog collar, with a name tag that read "Lump's Property." Every night, she had to perform on command, sucking his dick until he nutted, swallowing, eating his ass, taking it in every hole, until he was satisfied. When he was done, she had to wash him up like royalty, just like in that scene from *Coming to America* with Prince Akeem.

She spent hours at his feet, clipping his toenails, with a concentration that made her look almost serene, even though her mind was anything but. Each time she finished one foot, he would kick it away, muttering something demeaning, a reminder that this was her punishment, her penance. Lump would make her do the most degrading things, breaking her down piece by piece. And she endured it all, hoping that if she obeyed, he would forgive her, maybe even love her again.

One evening, as she knelt at the edge of the bed, clipping his toenails, Lump finally spoke. "You want my forgiveness?"

"Yes, King," Autumn nodded rapidly.

"Then you'll earn it. You'll earn it by findin' out where that bitch-ass nigga keeps his money," he said, his tone cold and detached. "Me and my Crimeys are gonna take everythang he's got. And when that's done, you're gonna put a bullet in his head. Before you do, you be sure to tell 'em why, too. You tell his ass he ain't shit, that you were runnin' game on 'em the entire time. That chu could never, ever be with a low vibrational ass nigga such as himself, and that chu only fuck with thoroughbred, boss ass niggaz. You got that?"

Autumn nodded, her voice a whisper. "Yes, King, anything you want."

"Good," he replied, leaning back in his chair. "Now get to work, bitch."

***

Days later...

After she delivered the information, Lump gathered his Crimeys, a ruthless band of Crips, made up of himself, Heavy, Grunt, and Whip. They were ready to hit Rolo where it hurt, and Lump knew this was his chance to take everything from the man who had dared to touch what was his. The streets were about to discover just how petty and vindictive Lump could be when crossed.

While Autumn kept Rolo occupied, the Crimeys hit the townhouse he had stashed up in Manhattan. They weren't sure who they'd find holding it down, maybe a couple of killaz standing guard, but instead, they ran into two pit bulls, thick as linebackers, veins bulging like they were juiced on steroids. The beasts were two of the meanest sons of bitches the homies had ever seen. Grunt and Whip wanted to put them down immediately, but Heavy stepped up, calm and confident.

"Nah, I got this," Heavy assured them. He knew a thing or two about pressure points and could handle a dog like a seasoned vet.

Lump, Grunt, and Whip kept the pits distracted, whistling and waving their arms, while Heavy snuck around to the back. After disabling the home security system, Heavy picked the lock on the back door and snuck inside, while the pits were focused on Lump, Grunt, and Whip. Heavy closed in on the dogs, then struck their pressure points with precise, swift blows. The beasts slumped to the ground, out cold.

With the hounds neutralized, Heavy unlocked the sliding glass door and waved his crime partners in. Grunt and Whip duct-taped the dogs' mouths and bound their legs, making sure they wouldn't get loose or make a sound. While they secured the pits, Lump assisted Heavy in cracking the safe in the back of Rolo's walk-in closet. Heavy opened his canvas bag, filled with tools for the trade, and got to work.

Grunt played lookout at the front, Whip at the back, while Lump stood behind Heavy like a scarecrow. Lump silently prayed that Heavy could crack this safe, like he'd cracked all the others. Judging by Rolo's flashy lifestyle, his bread, his jewelry, his mansions, and luxury cars, Lump estimated anywhere from three to five mil inside. So when Heavy finally swung the safe door open and they saw only

$500,000, the others were thrilled, but Lump's disappointment was written all over his face.

"The fuck is wrong with you, nigga? You not happy?" Whip asked, loading up the duffel bags with cash.

"Hell naw. Five hundred geez ain't shit." Lump kicked one of the bags, frustrated. He clenched and unclenched his leather-gloved hands, pacing back and forth, trying to keep his anger in check.

Whip grinned behind his ski mask. "Cuz, you needa calm yo' ass down and thank the good Lord above," he said, holding up stacks of money like a preacher waving a Bible.

Lump waved him off. "Man, I blow through that lil' bitta shit inna week's time. Fuck," He punched the air, imagining Rolo's face on the other side of his fists.

"Yo, cuz, calm that shit down before these rich-ass white niggaz call the Johnnies." Heavy was still on his knees, stuffing money into a duffle bag, but his eyes never left Lump.

Whip shrugged. "You trippin', Lump. Look at Grunt. Even he's happy." He nodded toward Grunt, who was smiling like he had a billion-dollar lottery ticket. "When have you ever seen this ugly-ass nigga smile?"

"Fuck you," Grunt shot back, flipping him off as he zipped up the last duffle bag.

"Maybe later," Whip joked, tucking the last of the cash inside.

Lump, still hot, muttered, "I want more. And I know that nigga's got it, so I'm gon' get it."

"Yeah? How?" Grunt asked as Heavy stood up, slinging a duffle bag over his shoulder.

***

Lump wasn't done. He wanted more than just half a mil, so after stashing the cash at his grandma's house, they headed to Rolo's baby mansion in Hell's Kitchen.

Whip parked the Mercedes-Benz station wagon in a shadowy corner of the neighborhood. Masked up, bulletproof vests strapped tight, and guns loaded, they ran up on the armed guards, their pistols chirping with each silenced shot. The guards howled in pain as bullets pelted them and they crumpled to the ground.

Grunt and Whip quickly dealt with the security system on the mansion's side, while Lump kept his eyes on Heavy, who was waiting at the front door, ready to pick the lock. Once Grunt gave the thumbs-up, Heavy worked his magic. In seconds, they were in.

Heavy stood, gun drawn, and led the way. The Crimeys fanned out, sweeping each room in search of Rolo. The sound of Jodeci's "Freek'N You" drifted down from upstairs, pulling them like a magnet toward the master bedroom. Heavy signaled for silence, leading the crew up the steps, each footfall was a whisper on the hardwood.

At the door, Lump took point, waited for the others to line up behind him, then kicked it in with the force of a cop raiding a trap house.

Rolo, mid-thrust, nearly jumped out of his skin, condom still dangling from his dick. Autumn scrambled, yanking a sheet up over her chest.

"Turn that bullshit off," Lump barked, snatching off his ski mask and storming toward Rolo. He glanced at Autumn, his eyes a storm of betrayal. She couldn't bring herself to look at him, so she fixed her gaze on the floor.

Rolo screamed like he caught his hand in a mousetrap as Lump yanked him off the bed by his hair. Heavy moved over to the cellphone, where the music blared, and smashed it with the butt of his gun until the noise died. He launched the shattered device against the wall and turned back to see Whip and Grunt duct-taping Rolo's wrists to the closet's pole.

Once they had him restrained, Lump went to work, slapping Rolo's face with his gun until blood flowed from cuts that quickly swelled into welts.

"I hope the pussy was worth it, dicksucka," Lump spat, glancing over his shoulder at Autumn, who was dressing hastily. He waved her over, pointing to where she should stand. She kept her eyes on the floor, avoiding Rolo's gaze.

Lump grabbed Rolo's chin roughly, forcing him to look up. Pressing his gun hard into Rolo's nut sack, he growled, "Listen, I'ma ask you one time, where's the money? And I don't mean them bullshit dummy safes you got for situations like this. I'm talkin' about the big boy safe, them millions, ya dig?"

Rolo's eyes rolled back; his face contorted in pain. Lump pressed harder. "Don't play with me, nigga. Tell me where it's at, or I'll blow yo' left nut off."

Once Rolo gave Lump the information he wanted, he turned to Grunt and Heavy. "Basement. Safe behind the washer. Combo is 12-19-09," he said, his voice low but clear, like they were sharing a secret they couldn't afford to forget.

Grunt and Heavy ran out of the room. They returned shortly with three duffle bags full of drug money.

Heavy, slightly winded, dropped the bags at Lump's feet and grinned. "Niggaz 'bouta eat good, cuz. Hadda be like four mil down there. No cap."

Lump looked at Grunt, who nodded in agreement, his face gleaming with satisfaction. Lump glanced at his timepiece and then back at Rolo, whose face was bruised and swollen from the beating. "It's time we shake the spot, my guy." He patted Rolo on the cheek, then pinched it like a grandma.

"Please, please, don't, don't kill me," Rolo pleaded weakly, barely conscious from the pistol-whipping. His voice was slurred, each word dragging out as if he were trying to hold onto his life just a little longer.

Lump stepped behind Autumn, placing his stick in her hands, and lifting it to meet Rolo's chest. "I'm not gon do

13

you in, bruh. I'ma let wifey do the honors. She's cold wit it, nah mean?" Lump gave Autumn a deep, sloppy, tongue kiss to rub the situation in Rolo's face. He then whispered in her ear, his voice a calm storm. "Now show this bitch-ass nigga who you truly belong to."

Autumn's eyes were glassy, her lips quivering as she mouthed, "I'm sorry," to Rolo, who begged her not to murk him. His body twisted against the closet's pole in a desperate attempt to escape.

She steadied her breath, her hands shaking slightly as she repeated the words Lump had told her to say the day she was clipping his toenails, "You ain't shit, nigga. I was runnin' game the entire time. I could never, ever be with a low vibrational ass nigga like you. I only fuck with thoroughbred, boss ass niggaz like my hubby."

Autumn took a deep breath and pulled the trigger. One shot pierced his heart, and a second exploded his skull against the closet wall in a gruesome spray of blood.

Lump kissed her again, his eyes filled with a twisted pride. "Good girl." He led her out of the bedroom, signaling for the crew to follow. Grunt, Heavy, and Whip grabbed the duffle bags and left the room behind him.

***

The Crimeys gathered in the basement of an old, abandoned house, with boarded windows and tall dead grass. This was their spot, where they always split the money, they made from their licks. Each man pulled out his own bag, stuffing it with his portion of the cash.

Heavy slapped hands with everyone, except Lump, who'd slipped upstairs to take a piss. "That nigga Lump went to take more than a leak," he said over his shoulder, insinuating that their crime partner was taking a shit. Everyone laughed heartily.

14

Heavy barely made it to the top of the steps, when the basement door creaked open, and a hushed bullet zipped through the air. He tumbled down the staircase, hard and fast, money flying everywhere. His body slammed into the ground and blood seeped out of his forehead.

Lump stood at the top of the stairs, the gun still hot in his hand, his eyes cold and calculating. He stared at Heavy's lifeless form for a moment, as if checking to see if the job was done. He nodded to Autumn, who quickly stuffed the scattered money back into Heavy's bag.

"Let's roll," Lump said, and the crew left the basement, stepping over Heavy's body as they climbed the stairs.

Heavy's eyes fluttered open, a low groan escaping his lips like he'd been resurrected. Blood blurred his vision, and his tongue felt thick in his mouth. He remembered seeing Lump's face before a bright white light flashed before his eyes.

The basement felt like hell, hot and suffocating, sweat pouring down his face. Heavy expected flames, a devil maybe, but then he heard his cellphone ring. He fumbled for it, catching it just as the call ended. He saw Shirvetta had called him sixty-seven times. He dialed 9-1-1, fingers shaking, and told the dispatcher his location and that he was in the basement. When she asked what happened, he hung up and called Shirvetta back.

"Baby, I got shot in the head," he croaked, voice weak. "If, if I don't make it, you, you raise the most vicious niggaz these streets have ever seen and sic 'em on Lump, Grunt, and Whip. No, no Johnnies, baby. Keep it, keep it gangsta."

Shirvetta's voice hitched in panic on the other end. Heavy tried to calm her, though his head swam in confusion and pain. "Don't worry, ambulance comin' for me," he said, but he wasn't so sure.

"Heavy. Heavy. Heavy," Shirvetta hysterically called after the love of her life, but it was already too late. The darkness had claimed him.

Heavy's eyelids fluttered open like the wings of a dying moth. His head throbbed, and the room spun slowly. He blinked several times, adjusting to the blinding white of the hospital lights. A thick patty had formed in his tightly coiled hair, and his facial hair was on the verge of turning into a full beard. The room around him was bursting with balloons, cards, and flowers, enough to make it look like a nursery. He tried to inhale the scent of a vase filled with daisies, but nothing came through. His sense of smell was gone.

Confusion clawed at his brain as he struggled to piece together fragments of time. What day was it? What year? The last time he'd been awake felt like an eternity ago. Then, it all slammed back into him like a brick wall. Lump. That muthafucka had shot him in the forehead and snatched his cut from the Rolo lick. His eyes narrowed into slits of pure hatred, the memory burning into his brain. *Those New York bitchez had probably been in on it too*, he thought. He vowed they'd all pay for not finishing the job.

Heavy tried to push himself out of bed, but hit the cold, hard floor like a stack of bricks. Pain shot through his body, but he gritted his teeth and forced himself to stand, stubborn as ever. It took a full hour for his legs to cooperate, trembling like a newborn foal's before he finally managed to get on his feet. He shuffled to the closet, pulling out the clear plastic bag containing the clothes he'd been shot in. He got dressed quickly, slipping on the bloodstained hoodie and throwing the hood over his head.

Next, he grabbed his cellphone, charger, and a small baggie, containing the money and everything he'd had in his pockets, from the nightstand drawer. He called a cab, then moved quietly to the door. At the nurses' station, a nurse was leaning over the counter, chatting with a colleague. She didn't notice Heavy slipping past, his steps light despite the pain in his limbs. He reached the elevator and punched the button, keeping his head low as it descended to the lobby.

When the doors opened, Heavy made his way across the room with his hood hiding his face. A security guard was too busy flirting with a visitor at the check-in desk to notice him. Heavy pushed through the glass doors and waited outside the hospital, his breath visible in the cold air. Within three minutes, the cab pulled up, and he climbed into the backseat.

The driver, an older Nigerian man, glanced back at him, frowning slightly.

"What day is it? What year?" Heavy asked, his voice raw.

The driver's eyebrows wrinkled in confusion. "It's November, 2014. Why you askin'?"

Heavy nodded. A month, give or take, since he'd been domed and jacked. He pulled out his cellphone to check in with his family, but the screen stayed black, dead. "You got a charger for this?" he asked, holding up his cellphone.

The driver nodded and took the phone, plugging it into the dashboard. Heavy stared out the back window, his thoughts dark until the driver announced they'd arrived at the destination. The old man handed the fully charged phone back, and Heavy passed him the fare, plus a tip.

"Thank you, sir," the driver said in his thick foreign accent, pocketing the cash with a nod.

Heavy slid out of the car, stepping into the yard of one of his family's many armories. He punched in a combination on the keypad and heard the lock click open. He stepped inside, the smell of gun oil and cold steel greeting him like an old friend. He geared up quickly, body armor, handguns, ammo, and a nickel-plated shotgun that gleamed under the dim light. His hands moved with practiced efficiency, fueled by the boiling anger inside him.

Once suited up, he tried calling Shirvetta, but it went straight to voicemail. "Damn," he muttered, pocketing the phone. He racked the shotgun and the sound echoed through the armory room. Without a second thought, he strode outside to the spare car in the backyard, a gun-metal gray '89 Chevy Camaro. He retrieved the key from its hiding spot behind the back tire, jumped in, and fired up the engine. The Camaro came back to life like the Frankenstein monster, and Heavy grinned, a flash of his pearly white teeth against his dark skin.

He peeled out of the yard, with a screech of tires. The car tore down the street like a missile on wheels. He had a score to settle, and he was ready to hand down some good old-fashioned street justice, one shell at a time.

***

Grunt and his boys were on one, riding high on a cocktail of cocaine and the best weed money could buy. French Montana's "Pop That" blasted through the surround sound, shaking the walls of the penthouse living room. Exotic dancers, half-naked and butt-naked, twisted and turned in every direction, their skin shimmering with sweat and champagne. Grunt's crew hooted and hollered, smacking asses and slapping twenties against jiggling flesh, making the bills stick like magic. They poured $500 bottles of Ace of Spades, drenching the dancers in golden showers of liquor, while the stench of smoke and sweat filled the air.

Grunt, chain heavy with gold and diamonds, threw himself onto a plush leather couch. His "Crimeys" cap was spun backward, and his eyes glistened with the manic energy of someone who'd seen too much and done too little. He took a deep swig from a bottle, wiping his mouth with the back of his hand, before reaching for a glass table covered in stacks of cash, pre-rolled blunts, and a neat line of cocaine, waiting for him like a lover. Just as he dipped the half-straw to snort, two dancers slid next to him, their eyes wide, lustful, and hungry for his high.

"You hoes can get some after I get mine," Grunt grinned, dipping down to the glass and inhaling the line with one swift motion. The coke hit him like a hammer, a rush of adrenaline flooding his senses. He leaned back, eyes closed, savoring the numbness spreading through his body. The dancer on his left snatched the straw from his hand and bent over to take her share, while the one on his right slid down, unzipping his designer jeans, and began working him over with her mouth.

Grunt's moans were low and guttural. "Yeah, shorty, slow, and real nasty, that's how a rich nigga like it." He ran his fingers through her hair, guiding her rhythm. His hips rose slightly off the couch, grinding into her face with every pass. The other dancer finished her toot and passed the straw, trading places with her partner. Her skills were next level. She had him gripping the couch cushions, his head thrown back, the tension in his muscles building as he teetered on the edge of euphoria.

Just as he was about to hit that sweet release, the front door exploded inward with a thunderous bang.

Boom.

A man wearing a blue bandana kicked it open like he owned the place, and everything fell apart in an instant. The music cut. Screams filled the air. Grunt's boys, and even a few of the strippers, scrambled for their guns, but the dude in the doorway was faster. Twin FNs flashed from his hands, spitting fire and metal into the room. He moved with military precision, a whirlwind of destruction, bullets flying in every direction. Grunt's boys dropped where they stood, their bodies crumpling to the floor in sprays of blood. The dancers scattered, shrieking, trying to find cover.

When the smoke cleared, silence hung thick, broken only by the sound of shell casings clinking to the floor. The living room was painted in red, bodies splayed out like discarded dolls. Only Grunt and his two dancers remained standing. The women had their hands up, shaking, covered in splattered blood, and trembling from the shock.

"Y'all bitches beat it. And turn off the music before you hit the door," the intruder barked, his voice cold and commanding.

The dancers grabbed whatever cash they could, turned off the music, and with a final glance of disgust at Grunt, fled out the door, promising themselves this was their last time dancing for a dead man walking.

As the door slammed shut, the man in the blue bandana yanked it down around his neck. Grunt's face twisted into a look of shock and fear, his eyes wide, as if he'd just seen a ghost. He tried to speak, but his voice caught in his throat.

"I thought, I thought you were dead," he whispered, unable to believe what he was seeing.

"I was dead," the man replied, his lips curling into a sinister smile. "But while I was in hell, I made a deal with the devil himself. He sent me back here to get what's mine." He lowered his guns to his sides, his gaze sweeping over the opulent room. Jet skis were stacked in the corner, big-screen TVs on every wall, an aquarium filled with exotic fish, and every gaming console imaginable. Expensive furniture and art littered the space, trophies of Grunt's ill-gotten gains.

Grunt's eyes darted to the MAC-10 on the coffee table, just a few inches away. His mind raced with options, calculating the odds.

The man in the bandana, now recognizable as Heavy, shook his head with disdain. "Look at all this shit you done bought witcho money, probably with some of mine, too," he sneered.

In a blink, Grunt lunged for the MAC-10. But Heavy was ready. He let loose a hail of bullets before Grunt's fingers even grazed the gun. Grunt convulsed as the bullets tore into him, his body jerking violently like a puppet on strings. Blood sprayed across the room, and he collapsed back onto the couch, wide-eyed, gasping for breath.

"You a stupid motherfucker, cuz," Heavy muttered, sitting down beside Grunt, who wheezed like he was sucking air through a straw. "I just wanted to ask you where I could find Whip. Checked his old spot, the place was cleaned out. Fuck." Heavy kicked the coffee table over in frustration, sending coke, money, and blunts flying. He looked back at Grunt, whose eyes had gone blank, his last breath rattling out of his chest.

A cellphone chimed from the kitchen, making Heavy whip around, his gun ready. He moved cautiously toward the sound and found a cellphone on the counter. The screen flashed with a photo of Grunt, grinning like an idiot, holding fat stacks of cash with two Puerto Rican baddies bent over a Bentley truck. The license plate read "1991."

Heavy chuckled, swiping up to unlock the phone, trying "1991" as the passcode. It worked. The screen unlocked, and there it was, a text thread with Whip. The messages were fresh, from just hours ago. Grunt had been trying to lure Whip to the party with promises of champagne, drugs, and more girls than he could handle. Whip had refused, saying he was too wasted to drive after hitting a Jamaican club, and had sent Grunt the address to his new spot instead.

Heavy's grin widened as he memorized the address. He pocketed the cellphone and quickly scanned the house for anything valuable. Scooping up stacks of cash and whatever jewelry he could find, he exited as silently as he had come. He disappeared into the night like a ghost, eyes fixed on his next target, vengeance burning hot in his veins.

***

Whip was down on his knees at his gold toilet, puking up his lungs. He'd made the mistake of mixing alcohol at the club earlier that night and now he was paying for it with interest. Whip wrapped up his business and brushed his teeth. Once he threw on all his icy jewelry and put the diamond earrings in his ear to impress the hoes upon their arrival, he texted Grunt, asking where he was as he descended the staircase. He was on his way to put up his pit-bull, Money, so he wouldn't frighten the girls when they came. The light above the stove was the only one shining inside the kitchen. Whip took like four steps before he slipped and landed on his side, grimacing.

"Aah, fuck, cuz." Whip held his aching side. Feeling something on his hands, he looked at them and they were coated in blood. Upon further inspection, he noticed his pitbull's head had been severed and he was lying in a pool of blood. He made an ugly face and was on the verge of tears, when he saw his dog's body. Crawling over to Money, he pulled its severed head and body into him and tried to put it back on, but it kept falling off, which made him cry like a baby. Hearing someone at his back, Whip drew his gun in one swift motion and pointed it at Heavy.

Bocka. Bocka. Bocka. Bocka.

Heavy ducked out of the doorway, taking two to the chest and one in the arm. Whip scrambled to his feet and checked his piece. Upping his gun, he slowly walked toward the living room, so he could finish the job he started. Whip placed his back against the doorway of the kitchen and took a few breaths before taking a peek and swinging in. Suddenly, Heavy kicked the gun out of his hands and turned his shotgun on him. He pulled its trigger and Whip launched backward in the kitchen. Whip's body bounced off the titanium refrigerator with a metallic thud, and he crumpled to the kitchen floor. The shotgun blast had ripped through his chest, a red stain blooming across his designer shirt, turning the white fabric dark and wet. His eyes fluttered open and shut, his breath coming in ragged, shallow gasps. Every inhale was a knife slicing through his lungs, every exhale was a desperate plea for life.

Heavy stepped over the splintered doorframe, chest heaving, shotgun still smoking in his hands. He winced as blood oozed from the bullet wound in his arm and stained his sleeve. He'd taken hits, but they were just flesh wounds, painful, but not enough to stop him. He walked toward Whip, his boots splashing through the blood-soaked floor, leaving crimson prints in his wake. He looked down at the pathetic scene. Whip, bleeding out, was still holding onto his mangled dog like some broken-hearted child.

"Look at chu," Heavy spat, his voice a low growl. "Cryin' over a goddamn dog. Now I bet two inches of my dick, you didn't shed 'nan tear when Lump popped my ass in the head. Did you?" Whip just stared up at him. "I thought so."

Whip coughed, a wet, hacking sound that sent fresh spurts of blood from his lips. He tried to push himself up, but his arms gave out, and he collapsed back onto the floor. "You, you ain't gonna get away with this, Heavy," he wheezed, his voice barely a whisper.

Heavy laughed, a cold, hollow sound that echoed through the kitchen. "Ain't nobody left to stop me, nigga. Yo' crew 'bouta be gone. Grunt's dead. And now yo' ass 'bouta join 'em."

Whip's eyes flickered with fear, but he tried to put on a brave front. "I got people, man. I got connections. They'll find you," he muttered, his voice breaking with each word. "They'll make sho' you pay for this."

Heavy shook his head, a smirk creeping onto his lips. "Nah, Whip. You ain't got nobody now. All your people are either dead or too scared to come for me. I ain't worried about no fuckin' connections."

Heavy raised the shotgun again, pointing it straight at Whip's face. Whip's eyes widened, his breathing quickening as he stared down the barrel. His mind raced, searching for any way out, any last words that could buy him even a second more of life.

"Please, please, Heavy," he whispered, tears in his eyes.

Heavy's smirk widened into a full grin. "Youz a gangsta, right? Well, be gangsta, don't start bitching up now."

Whip's lips trembled, his mouth opening and closing like a fish out of water. He looked up at Heavy, his eyes filled with fear and hatred. "You gonna, you gonna burn in hell for this," he croaked, his voice breaking.

Heavy's smile disappeared, his face hardening into a mask of fury. "Then I'll see you there."

Bloom.

The blast echoed through the kitchen, drowning out Whip's last scream. The back of Whip's head exploded against the stainless steel refrigerator, leaving a splatter of blood and brain matter like a grotesque painting. His body went limp, eyes staring blankly at the ceiling, mouth frozen in a final scream that never came.

Heavy lowered the shotgun, breathing heavily, feeling the pain in his chest and arm throbbing with every heartbeat. He looked around the blood-drenched kitchen, his eyes landing on the severed bulldog's head and body lying in a pool of its own blood. For a moment, he felt a pang of regret, not for Whip, but for the innocent dog caught in the crossfire of this brutal vendetta.

He shook his head, forcing the thought away. No time for sympathy, no room for pity. Not in this life. Not with what he had to do. He reached into Whip's pocket and pulled out a set of keys, knowing they would lead him to something valuable. Then, with one last glance at the bloody scene, he turned and limped out of the kitchen, stepping over Whip's lifeless body.

He didn't stop until he reached the front door. Heavy paused, took a deep breath, and stepped out into the cold night, disappearing into the darkness. His mission wasn't over yet. He had one more name on his list, Lump.

***

Autumn walked through the door after a long day of shopping on Fifth Avenue, her arms filled with luxury bags from the finest stores. Her low crooning filled the entryway as she danced over the threshold, her joy evident in every step. She bumped the door closed with her hips, locked all the locks, and made her way toward the staircase, thoughts drifting to the comfort of her bedroom.

But before she could take more than a few steps, a cold, menacing voice shattered her sense of safety.

"Aaaaaah!" Autumn's eyes widened in terror as she screamed, dropping her bags in a flurry of expensive fabric and leather. Her heart pounded as she fumbled for the .380 pistol her in her purse.

"Slow yo' roll, lil' mama, 'fore I blow yo' fuckin' wig off," the voice snarled from the staircase, where Heavy stood, his imposing figure partially hidden in the shadows. His nickel-plated shotgun gleamed ominously in the dim light, trained directly on her.

Terrified, Autumn froze, her hand falling away from her purse, trembling as she raised both hands in surrender. The fear was written all over her face, tears beginning to well up in her eyes.

"That's a good bitch," Heavy sneered, the threat in his voice leaving no room for doubt. He approached her slowly, the shotgun still aimed at her, his eyes cold and intimidating. Without breaking eye contact, he snatched her purse and dumped its contents onto the floor, scattering makeup, a wallet, and her cellphone across the hardwood. Using his foot, he sifted through the mess until he found what he was looking for, her cellphone.

Heavy picked up the phone and scrolled through her contacts until he found Lump's name. He grinned, a cruel, twisted expression, as he pressed the call button. Autumn stood before him, silently crying, her body trembling uncontrollably as she watched him with wide, terrified eyes.

"Nah, nigga, it ain't yo' bitch, it's Karma. I suggest you bring yo' ol' busta ass home with the rest of that chili 'fore I blow her ass down," Heavy growled into the phone, his eyes never leaving Autumn's tear-streaked face.

On the other end of the line, Lump's voice was filled with panic. "I swear to God, cuz, if you hurt my wife…" But before he could finish, Heavy kicked Autumn hard in the stomach. She doubled over in pain, clutching herself as she gasped for air, only for Heavy to backhand her viciously with the hand holding her cellphone. The force of the blow sent her crashing to the floor, where she lay unconscious, a small trickle of blood oozing from her temple as she began snoring loudly.

"And did," Heavy said coldly before disconnecting the call. He tossed the cellphone somewhere far across the room and slid Autumn's .380 into his pocket. Propping his shotgun against the wall, he methodically went to work, dragging a chair from the living room. He lifted Autumn's limp body and duct-taped her to the chair, binding her hands and ankles efficiently.

He then duct-taped a plastic bag over her head. Every breath she took fogged up the plastic, the condensation building until the bag began to glisten with moisture. The effect was suffocating, a slow, torturous reminder of the fragility of life.

With Autumn secured and unconscious, Heavy picked up his shotgun and slid her chair back against the bottom of the staircase. He sat down behind her, the shotgun resting across his lap as he settled in to wait for Lump's arrival.

***

Lump eased his 2006 BMW 325i to a halt outside his house, the engine purring softly before he turned it off. He stepped out, tucking his gun into the waistband of his jeans, and retrieved a briefcase from the trunk. His mind was on autopilot as he approached the front door, intent on dealing with whatever awaited him inside.

He was about to knock on the front door when he heard Heavy's voice, echo from within. "It's open, fuck boy."

Lump pushed the door open, stepping inside, he immediately froze. Autumn was struggling for breath, a

26

plastic bag duct-taped over her head, her movements slow and jerky, on the edge of suffocation. Lump took a step toward her, but Heavy, standing next to her, calmly tore a hole in the bag with his finger. Autumn gulped in the air desperately, her head tilting back, lungs working overtime to fill themselves with oxygen.

Lump's eyes were wide, fear and fury dancing across his face. "What the fuck, cuz? I told you I was comin'. You was gon' fuckin' kill her anyway?" His voice cracked as he spoke. He'd put her through hell since catching her messing around with his connect, but he hadn't stopped loving her. He never wanted to see her dead.

Heavy grinned, his shotgun unwavering in his hand. "I wasn't bullshittin' when I said hurry yo' bitch-ass home. You lucky you made it in time, nigga. Otherwise, this bitch woulda been making nice with Rolo again, in the afterlife."

Lump swallowed, rage bubbling beneath his calm exterior. "Whatever, cuz. I brought the money." He opened the briefcase, the crisp bills catching the light. Heavy's eyes flickered with greed for a split second, but the dark, malevolent glint quickly returned.

"We good?" Lump asked, snapping the case shut and sitting it on the floor.

Heavy's smile faded, replaced by a menacing stare. "Nah."

Frustration boiling over, Lump snapped and threw up his hands in frustration. "Then what the fuck else do you want, man?"

"Yo life."

Heavy's shotgun roared, and Lump felt something hot rip through the muscles of his abdomen. He staggered back, body folding forward as the pain went through him. Before he could cry out, Heavy's shotgun had something else to say.

Bloom.

The blast blew apart the top half of Lump's skull, splattering blood and chunks of meat against the wall behind him. His body hit the floor with a sickening thud. His eyes were vacant and his face was frozen in shock.

Heavy turned his attention to Autumn, her breath coming in panicked gasps. Slipping behind her, he pulled the barrel of the shotgun against her throat, violently choking her. Her eyes widened in terror, unable to lessen the pressure applied to her windpipe, due to her wrists being bound. The veins in her neck bulged, her face turned red as she struggled to breathe, tears flowed down her cheeks. Heavy didn't relent. He pulled harder, her body convulsed as the life drained from her, until finally, she went limp.

He released her, letting her slump back in the chair. Dropping the shotgun with a clatter, Heavy picked up the briefcase. He glanced around the room one last time and a satisfied smirk spread across his lips as he walked out the door.

But as Heavy disappeared into the night, he remained blissfully unaware of the hidden security cameras capturing his every move. Those cameras had seen it all, the murder, the cold-blooded execution of a man and his wife.

He thought he was in the clear. But Heavy didn't know the whole thing had been caught on the hidden security cameras Lump had installed, every second of his sins recorded, every brutal act on display. It was only a matter of time before the cops came knocking. And when they did, there'd be no escape, no way out for Heavy.

The devil always gets his due.

Chapter 1

The basement was so quiet all they could hear was the ticking of the clock on the wall and the buzzing of a fly, swarming around aimlessly. Golden didn't bat an eye as he waited for his mother's response, alongside the twins. His heart started racing like he'd eaten an edible, and he found himself having a little trouble breathing.

"Alright, you wanna know if I killed yo' brother's mother or not? The answer is yes," Shirvetta admitted, stunning everyone around her. "Yes. I killed that bitch. And had I not done what I did, we wouldn't have the family we have now."

"Ma, noooo." Baby Girl looked at her mother in disbelief.

Biggie couldn't say shit. The revelation was like a punch to his gut, and he felt like the wind had been knocked out of him.

Golden stared at Shirvetta, seething, nostrils flared, lips twisted, tears dripping from his eyes.

"Oh, don't look at me like that, Golden," Shirvetta scrunched her face. She couldn't believe her children had the reaction they had when she'd done what she did for them. "Chick had yo' daddy under her spell. I knew he'd never let her go unless she was outta the picture. You know what? I'll be damn if I sit here and let y'all make me feel bad, when I did right by y'all. Y'all should be lined up to kiss my ass right now 'cause it's 'cause of me you had a full time daddy in ya life."

"I can't believe you, ma. I need a drink." Baby Girl shot to her feet, storming over to the bar to make herself a drink. She tapped her foot heatedly as she tossed back the alcohol and poured herself another shot.

"Boy, I wasn't ready for this shit tonight. I need a cigarette, and bad, too," Shirvetta said to no one in particular, taking a pack of Newports from inside of her homemade sling. She placed a cigarette between her lips and requested a light from Biggie. After he obliged her request, she took a hit and blew out a cloud of smoke. She swept her hair out of her face and looked at Golden. He looked like a raging beast, who couldn't wait to be let out of its cage.

"Pop, are you there? Pop?" Biggie picked up Golden's cellphone. "He hung up," he announced, looking from his brother to his mother. He could tell Golden was dealing with a bout of emotional turmoil.

Shirvetta took the cigarette out of her mouth and blew a cloud of smoke. "Why are you lookin' at me like that?"

Golden opened his mouth to say something, but his feelings choked him. He took the time to gather himself before trying to speak again. "You fucked up Cowboy's life. He's all screwed up now, and it's all 'cause of you." Tears collected in his eyes and rolled down his face. "My big brother is broken so bad, I don't know if I can even fix 'em, but I'm gonna try. I'm never gonna give up on 'em."

Golden grabbed his helmet and pocketed his cellphone. He started up the staircase but turned around when his mother called after him.

Shirvetta pulled herself up from the couch with her walking cane. "You only get one mother, son. I want chu to remember that."

Golden glared at her for a moment and continued up the staircase.

"Sis, pour me a shot, would ya?" Biggie asked Baby Girl. He walked toward the bar beside his mother, in case she needed his assistance. As soon as they sat at the bar, Baby Girl gave them both a shot each.

Shirvetta watched her youngest children throw back the shots of alcohol. Baby Girl refilled the glasses and they carried on like she wasn't even there. Shirvetta was expecting them to come at her with a barrage of questions, and it was driving her up the wall that they hadn't."Okay. Come on with it." Shirvetta blew out smoke and mashed her cigarette out on the bar top. The twins looked at her with clueless expressions on their faces. "About me closin' the curtains on Cowboy's biological mother's show."

"There really ain't much more to say, ma. You know what chu did is messed up, and so do Biggie and I," Baby Girl said. She was still trying to figure out how to handle the news. If it hadn't come from her own mother's lips that she bodied her oldest brother's mother, then she would have never believed it.

Shirvetta turned to Biggie. "And you?"

Biggie took a breath and slumped his shoulders. "Like Baby Girl said, what chu did to bruh moms is messed up. I know if I was in bro's shoes, I'd be plottin' how to do you in. Real talk."

"Oh, best believe that's exactly what that crazy mothafucka's doin', plottin'," Shirvetta assured him. "You heard what Golden said he told 'em, that was clearly a threat. Can we all agree on that?" She looked at the twins and they nodded in agreement. "Good. Look, I'm on the injured list right now, so it's gonna be up to y'all two to get this thing done." Baby Girl's forehead wrinkled. "Get what thing done?"

"I think we all know what I'm talkin' about here, but if you need me to come out and say it, I will," Shirvetta said. "You two are gonna take out Cowboy."

"Ma, are you serious?" Baby Girl asked.

"Oh, yes I am, so I need you to take this situation just like that, seriously," Shirvetta replied. She then turned to Biggie, rubbing the back of his head. "How about it, baby boy? Can I count on you?"

Biggie reluctantly nodded. After popping all that shit about killing Cowboy, now that he got the greenlight, he had cold feet. He knew his mother's life was in danger, as long as Cowboy was alive, and if push came to shove, he would use his love for her to carry out his execution.

"I hate to put it to you like this, sweetie, but you're gonna have to make a choice," Shirvetta started back up with Baby Girl. "Now it's either gonna be me or ya brother. If I were you, I'd choose me 'cause even with junior gone, you'll still have two brothers left."

Baby Girl looked at her mother in shock. She couldn't believe what she'd just said to her. It was fucked the fuck up, but she was absolutely right. She had to make a choice.

"So, what's it gonna be?" Shirvetta asked. She looked upon her with pleading eyes, hoping she'd be down with the assassination.

Baby Girl bowed her head and big teardrops fell from her eyes. She wiped them away and looked back up at Shirvetta, nodding.

"That's my girl. I knew you wouldn't let cho mother down." Shirvetta grinned, reaching across the bar and hugging her with her good arm. She kissed her forehead, turned to Biggie, and gave him the same form of affection.

***

Heavy splashed water on his face and stared at his reflection in the metal reflector. The past had finally come back to bite him in his ass. He didn't have any idea how he was going to handle his situation, so he figured it was best he slept on it. He laid down on his mattress with his fingers interlocked behind his head. He knew, without a doubt, there was going to be one hell of a war on the streets, and unfortunately, it was going to be waged between his children. What was even more fucked up was he wasn't free to stop the war from happening. His only hope was that Golden could stop his blood from spilling its own blood. It was a long shot, but it was the only way he could see the issue being resolved.

I know it's a lot for you to deal with, youngin', but I pray to God that you can pull it off.

***

Chris Stacks' nurse threw a big towel and a washcloth over her shoulder and picked up the bassinet of sudsy hot water. She walked down the corridor singing softly.

"Where you going, Mercy?" one of the nurses asked as she passed her.

"To give my patient a bath," Nurse Mercy replied.

"Oh. Well, have fun," the nurse said, turning left at the end of the hallway.

Nurse Mercy walked inside Chris Stacks' room and flipped on the light switch. She pulled the curtain back and his bed was empty. But it still held the mold of his body. Nurse Mercy dropped the bassinet and sudsy water spilled everywhere. She looked under the bed and checked the bathroom, but he wasn't there either. She slipped on the water she spilt running toward the door, but scrambled back upon her sneakers. Running out into the corridor, she hollered for the attention of the rest of the hospital staff on her wing.

***

The elevator stopped on the garage floor and its double doors opened. Hush, who was wearing a mask and blue scrubs over his mouth, emerged pushing a wheelchair with Chris Stacks slumped in it. He had on a big straw hat and a blanket was draped over him. He slowly came out of his coma as he was rolled through the parking lot. Frowning, he lifted his head and stared at the blurry image in front of him. As his vision came back to normal, so did what was before his eyes. It was Boodee standing at the rear of the Suburban, smoking a cigarette. When he saw Chris Stacks, he dropped the burning cancer stick at his foot and mashed it out. He then opened the back door of the truck and stood aside so Chris could get in.

Chris Stacks didn't know who the fuck Boodee was, so he knew his situation couldn't be good. He thrashed around in the wheelchair, trying desperately to get out, but to no avail. His wheelchair suddenly stopped, and Hush stepped in front of him, pulling his mask down.

"You can try as hard as you want, but yo' ass ain't gettin' outta this one," Hush told him and snatched off the blanket like he was revealing something. Chris Stacks had duct tape over his mouth, and his wrists and ankles were duct taped to the wheelchair. He threw his head back, trying to scream for help, and his hat fell off.

Hush punched him in the chin and knocked him out cold. He then motioned Boodee over. "Help me get this muthafucka in the backseat, B."

Boodee cut the duct tape from Chris Stacks' wrists and ankles, and then pocketed his Swiss army knife. Hush grabbed him underneath his arms while Boodee grabbed hold of his legs. After they deposited him into the backseat, they hopped inside the Suburban and drove out of the garage.

Chapter 2

The last time Golden was laid up with Aries he placed a tracking application on her cellular so he'd know where she was at all times. He was hoping Aries would have bodied Rich Loc so he wouldn't have to use the app, but unfortunately, things didn't work out that way.

Golden parked his car in the backyard of his parent's house and pulled out his Kawasaki Ninja 400 motorcycle. He slipped his helmet over his head, adjusted it, and turned the key in the ignition. The bike came to life, and he revved it up. It squealed annoyingly loud. He took off down the driveway, made a right at the end of it, and zipped up the block.

Golden made it back to the armory, where he'd stashed his money from the Rich Loc lick and got dressed in a black leather motorcycle suit. He went into the small study, pulled a thick green book downward, and the bookshelf slid back inside the wall. A neon blue light popped on, revealing a room loaded with a cache of weapons hanging on every wall. Entering the room, Golden took his time looking over the variety of guns, like they were the blueprint to some sort of machine he planned to build. He found the weapon he was looking for and took it down, checking the sights on it. It was a modified P-90 Herstal submachine gun. He also strapped a bowie knife to his thigh and strapped a holstered .380 semi-automatic pistol to his ankle.

Golden took one more look at his cellphone for Aries's location as he stepped out of the house. He slipped his cell back inside his pocket, shut the visor of his helmet, and mounted his Kawasaki Ninja. He flew down the block, leaving debris in his wake.

***

"A'ight, shorty, I'm finna get outta here. Gemme a kiss," Rich Loc tucked his gun at the small of his back and pulled her close. Aries cupped his face and kissed him twice.

"I love you," Aries told him.

"I love you, too. Don't forget to drop that package off to Rollins," Rich Loc replied, picking up the duffle bags. Parelli was driving him around to the families of the locs who lost their lives so he could give them enough dough for themselves and to pay for their loved ones' funerals.

"I won't."

Aries shut the front door behind him and locked it. She walked back toward the master bedroom to get dressed and spotted Rich Loc's keys on the dining room table. Snatching his keys, she ran out onto the front porch, but Rich Loc was already gone. Walking back inside the house, she sent him a text to let him know he'd forgotten his keys. Afterward, she got dressed, wrapped up half of a kilo, and placed it inside her oversized designer purse. Hearing someone honking outside, she figured it was Rich Loc coming back to retrieve his keys.

"That man would forget his head if it wasn't attached to his neck." Aries smiled, grabbing the shopping bag and Rich Loc's keys. She walked back to the front of the house and looked through the curtains to make sure it was Rich Loc outside.

***

Golden sped through the New York City streets, like he had the road all to himself. He cut it close, tailgating, and dipping in and out of lanes. Coming off the highway, he slowed to the speed limit and made his way to his destination. He stopped his motorcycle outside of Rich Loc's crib, drew his P-90 Herstal submachine gun, and blew his horn. He pointed his weapon at the window he believed Rich Loc would look out from and waited for him to appear. As soon as the curtain was pulled back from the window, Golden squeezed the trigger and a burst of flames spat out of his weapon's barrel.

The window exploded in a shower of glass as the gun's muzzle flashing lit up the night. He dismounted his motorcycle, the submachine gun still hot in his hands, and charged the porch. With a powerful kick, he sent the front door flying off its hinges and splinters of wood scattering everywhere.

As soon as Golden ran inside the house, his adrenaline-fueled rage vanished when he saw Aries lying on the floor, her eyes wide and filled with tears. Blood gushed from her wounds, and her mouth, staining the floor a deep red. Golden's heart beat violently in his chest. He had fucked up bad.

He had come for Rich Loc, but instead, he had shot up his lady. The realization hit him like a freight train and the air left his lungs in a guttural cry. He dropped to his knees beside Aries, his hands trembling as he cradled her head.

"No, no, no," he repeated with his voice breaking. "I'm sorry. I'm so sorry."

He fumbled for her cellphone, his fingers slick with her blood. Dialing 9-1-1, he tried to steady his shaking voice. "Please, send an ambulance. Hurry," he choked out the address with frantic urgency.

Aries coughed weakly and blood bubbled over her lips. She placed her shaky hand against his chest. Her eyes, once full of life and love, now reflected pain and regret.

"Save yo' strength," Golden urged her, tears spilling down his cheeks.

She ignored his advice though. She was persistent. Her voice came out in a weak whisper. "I-I-I l-love y-you," Aries managed, her words faltering as tears slid down her cheeks.

Golden's heart shattered into a billion pieces. The distant wail of sirens grew louder, and the urgency of his situation crashed over him. He wanted to stay, to hold her and beg for her forgiveness, but to do so would be risking his incarceration. "I have to go," he whispered before kissing her forehead tenderly. He laid her head gently on the floor and stood, picking up his submachine gun.

With one last, heart-wrenching glance at Aries, he ran to the front door. Pausing with one foot out, he looked back at the woman he loved, her life slipping away before his eyes. Every instinct screamed at him to stay, hold her hand, and keep her safe, but he knew he'd be sealing his fate if he did.

"I love you," he whispered, voice cracking with raw emotions.

Frustration and despair fought within Golden as he slammed his fist against the doorway. Mounting his motorcycle, he glanced over his shoulder at the flashing emergency lights closing in. The sound of the police car sirens was a harsh reminder of the consequences that were bearing down on him. Revving the engine, he zipped down the street and popped a wild wheelie. He then brought his front wheel down and tore out of the neighborhood, leaving behind his future wife and the life he had destroyed.

***

Golden's visor caught every flicker of the city lights as he tore through the streets, the roar of his motorcycle matching the chaos in his mind. His grip tightened on the handlebars, teeth clenched as he narrowly dodged between cars. *I shot her.* The words echoed like a curse. If Aries didn't make it, he wasn't sure how he'd live with himself.

As the road blurred beneath him, he took a sharp turn, pulling up next to a storm drain in a deserted corner. His head snapped around, scanning for any eyes on him. None. He unstrapped the machine gun slung across his back, the weight of it suddenly unbearable, and let it drop to the ground. With a hard kick, the weapon clattered into the drain, disappearing into the void. No turning back now.

Golden revved the engine and gunned it toward the family junkyard. This wasn't the first time he'd needed something to vanish, and the old man running the joint had been doing dirty work for the Loves for years. The deal was quick and silent, cash exchanged for discretion. Within minutes, the crusher's iron jaws came down on his motorcycle, reducing it to a twisted hunk of metal, unrecognizable.

He didn't waste any time. Heading straight to the restroom, Golden stripped out of the motorcycle suit, helmet included, and stuffed everything into a garbage bag. His heart pounded in his chest as he tied it off, knowing that every second counted. With a brisk pace, he left the yard and ducked into a narrow alleyway a few blocks down. The flick of his lighter sparked in the darkness; the flame hungry as it consumed the bag. Smoke curled into the night sky, and as the suit burned away, so did the evidence of everything he'd done.

Without looking back, Golden slipped out of the alley and flagged down a yellow cab. He slid into the backseat, his pulse still racing. The cabbie didn't ask questions as Golden gave him the address of one of the family armories. Within minutes, he was out, swapping into fresh clothes, shedding every trace of the killer he had been a few hours ago.

Golden slid behind the wheel of his ride and fired it up. Reversing out of the driveway, he swung out into the middle of the residential street and mashed the gas, speeding toward the hospital he hoped and prayed they had taken Aries to.

Tears debuted in his eyes as his guilt twisted in his chest like the bayonet on an old rifle.

She has to make it, Golden thought, pressing the pedal to the metal. There was no room for anything else in his mind now. Aries was his top priority. If she didn't pull through, little else mattered.

Chapter 3

Rich Loc felt the exhaustion weighing down on his muscles as he leaned back in the chair. It had been a long, grueling day, and this was the last stop. The last person on his list of families to visit, the last loved one of the men he'd lost in the brutal firefight at the auto shop.

He sat across from a young woman, the mother of Grip's child, as she rocked the four-month-old baby in her arms. The baby, blissfully unaware of the tragedy that had struck, slept soundly against her chest. Her eyes were red and swollen, rimmed with the glassy-pink of relentless tears. Her cheeks were slick with fresh streaks of grief, and her nose was raw, rubbed red from countless swipes with a tissue. She'd been crying since he arrived, the weight of her sorrow hanging heavy in the room like a storm cloud.

Rich Loc had been here before, too many times. He knew the words to say, the tone to take. He leaned forward, his voice low and gravelly, "Grip was a stalwart soldier. You know that, right? Loyal, dependable, fierce, there ain't no one out there like him. If I could, I'd trade places with him in a heartbeat, just so you and that little one wouldn't have to feel this pain."

The young woman's tears fell anew as his words settled over her, like a shroud. She clutched the baby tighter to her chest, her shoulders trembling. Rich Loc kept his expression neutral, though inside, the guilt gnawed at him. It was the same routine at every house, lay it on thick, let the family break down, and then leave them with enough money to ease their burden. It was the least he could do, the only thing he could do.

Diamond, silent and watchful, stood by Rich Loc's side as he reached into the duffle bag at his feet. One by one, he placed thick stacks of cash on the worn kitchen table, the thud of each pile the only sound in the room besides the woman's quiet sobs. The cash stacked higher and higher, until it resembled a small building, a fortress of currency meant to shield Grip's family from the harsh realities of life without him.

When the bag was empty, Rich Loc slid it to Diamond, who wordlessly slung it over his shoulder. Then, Rich Loc turned his attention back to the young woman. She was adjusting the strap of her tank top, pulling it back up to cover her exposed, sagging breast. Her eyes, hollow with grief, met his.

"I've already taken care of the funeral arrangements," Rich Loc informed her with a steady voice, gesturing toward the money between them. "This right here, this is just a lil' something to make sure you and the baby are taken care of. When it runs out, hit me up, you hear? Grip was a loyal dude, and the least I can do is make sho' his family is good."

He reached into his pocket and pulled out a card, handing it to her. She took it with trembling fingers, then collapsed against him, wrapping one arm around his shoulders, the baby still cradled in the other. Her tears soaked into his shirt as she thanked him over and over, her voice a choked whisper.

"No need to thank me," Rich Loc murmured, his hand gently patting her back. "Grip's service was more than enough. You've got my number. Don't hesitate to use it when you need me. I mean that." He held her by the shoulders and looked into her eyes, making sure she understood. Then, he hugged her one last time, before she led him and Diamond to the front door.

Outside, J-Bo was waiting by the car, his hands crossed at his waist, near his strap. His eyes scanned the street for any signs of trouble. He nodded to Rich Loc as they approached, his gaze lingering briefly on Grip's baby mama before he turned and opened the car door.

"Stay safe, shorty," Rich Loc said to her, giving a final nod as he slid into the back seat.

She waved goodbye as she watched J-Bo back out of the driveway.

***

The car was silent as they drove through the city, the tension in the air thick as they made their rounds, dropping off cash and condolences to the families of the fallen. By the time they finished, the sun had dipped below the horizon, leaving the sky a dark, bruised purple. Hunger gnawed at them, a reminder that they hadn't eaten all day, so they decided to hit up Denny's before heading back to Rich Loc's crib.

The diner was nearly empty, the hum of fluorescent lights and the clatter of silverware were the only recurring sounds. Rich Loc, thoughts elsewhere, absentmindedly picked at his food. J-Bo and Diamond's voices were low and animated as they swapped stories about the families they visited.

"You see Grip's baby mama?" Diamond said, shaking his head with a sly grin. "Man, she's thick as hell. Couldn't keep my eyes off her."

"Yeah, no kidding," J-Bo added, chuckling. "Bet Grip had his hands full with that one."

Rich Loc looked up sharply, his eyes narrowing. "Cut that shit out," he said, his tone cold and final. "Show some respect."

The laughter died instantly, and both men fell silent, their eyes dropping to their plates. Rich Loc shook his head, calling for the waitress to bring a few containers for the leftovers. As she walked off to get them, he pulled out his cellphone and tried calling Aries again, the knot in his stomach tightening when it went straight to voicemail. He'd tried her a few times earlier, to check in, but she hadn't picked up then either. It wasn't like her to ignore his calls, and now, unease prickled at the edges of his thoughts.

The waitress returned with the containers, and Rich Loc quickly packed up the food, anxious to get back home. The drive felt longer than it should have, every red light testing his patience, every passing minute feeding his worry.

When they finally pulled up to his house, Rich Loc's heart sank. The front yard was ablaze with red and blue lights, the flashes reflecting off the neighboring houses like an ominous beacon. Police cars were parked haphazardly along the curb, and an unmarked sedan that Rich Loc recognized as belonging to a detective was in the driveway. The front door of his house hung open, the night breeze stirring the bloodstained curtains.

Panic surged through him. Aries. His mind raced with possibilities, each more terrifying than the last. Had she been busted with the package? Had something gone wrong with the deal? The calls from Rollins, who she was supposed to meet, now seemed like warnings he had failed to heed.

Without waiting for J-Bo to stop the car, Rich Loc threw open the door and ran toward the house. A uniformed officer stepped in his path, outstretching his hand to stop his advance.

"Who are you?" the officer demanded with a sharp tone.

"This is my house," Rich Loc snarled, shoving past him. The smell of blood hit him like a punch to the mouth as he stepped inside, his eyes taking in the scene, bloodstains on the carpet and shattered glass. "Aries," he shouted, his voice echoing off the walls. "Aries?"

Another officer tried to hold him back, but Rich Loc shoved him aside, his desperation driving him forward. He had to find her, had to know she was okay.

A man in a blazer, the detective from the driveway, approached him, holding up his hand to calm him.

"Relax," the detective said, voice dripping with the kind of false sympathy that made Rich Loc want to break his nose. "Aries has been shot. She was rushed to the hospital."

Rich Loc's blood ran cold. "How bad is it? Which hospital?" he demanded, his voice a low growl.

The detective shrugged and took a sip of his coffee. "Don't know. They just took her. That's all I got."

Rich Loc didn't wait for more. He turned on his heel and sprinted out of the house, heart hammering in his chest. He barely registered the concerned looks from J-Bo and Diamond as he jumped into his car and peeled out of the driveway, tires screeching against the pavement. He had to get to Aries. He had to make sure she was okay.

God help whoever was responsible, if she wasn't.

***

Golden signed in at the hospital, barely holding it together as he grabbed the visitor's pass and slapped it on his chest. He hopped on the elevator in the lobby and got off on the fifth floor. Dashing around the corner, he ran into a doctor coming out of Aries' room.

"Hello, Doctor Lombardi," Golden addressed him by the name on his badge, shaking his hand. "I'm Maurice, Aries' cousin," he lied smoothly. "How is she doing?"

"She got out of surgery about," Lombardi glanced at his wristwatch, "an hour and a half ago. She should be fine. Unfortunately, the bullets that entered her caused some serious nerve damage to her spine. So, she won't be able to feel anything from the neck down, nor will she ever walk again."

Golden felt like Gervonta Davis punched him in the kidney. His world spun off its axis. His vision narrowed and the weight of everything crashed down on his shoulders.

Growling, he unleashed a flurry of punches on the nearest wall before collapsing to his hands and knees, breaking down sobbing. Nurses and patients watched in shock as he threw a full-blown tantrum, the kind that would've gotten him kicked out of any other place. Security was ready to rush him, but Doctor Lombardi stepped in just in time, telling them to stand down.

A couple of nurses approached Golden, their voices soft as they tried to soothe him, offering comforting words until he slowly gathered himself. His eyes were red, his breathing shallow, but he knew he had to pull it together, at least for Aries. He headed to the restroom and splashed cold water on his face, trying to get rid of the evidence of his meltdown.

When he finally walked into Aries's room, his chest tightened at the sight of her. There she was, his girl, lying in bed, wearing an oxygen mask, an IV, and tubes leading to and from her. Golden's mind played tricks on him, and for a second, he swore he saw her in a coffin. His breath hitched, panic setting in as he squeezed his eyes shut and tried to block out the horrifying image.

Nah, bro, nah. That ain't it. That ain't real.

When he opened his eyes again, the vision was gone.

Golden scanned the room and found a clock on the wall. He'd heard that you couldn't see clocks in dreams, and the ticking hands grounded him back to reality. Relieved, he approached her bedside slowly, as if walking too fast might shatter her fragile body. He glanced at the door to make sure no one was around before leaning in close, his voice cracking.

"It was me, baby. It was me," he choked out, his face contorted in agony. "I shot chu. I fuckin' shot chu. I'm sorry, ma. I'm so sorry." His voice broke, and he collapsed onto her, his face pressed against hers. He clung to her, sobbing so hard he could barely breathe, tears soaking into her pillow. But after a while, even his body ran out of tears.

Sniffling, he wiped his nose with his sleeve and sat up. His voice was hoarse when he spoke again. "I'm gonna grab a cup of ice. I'll be right back, mamas. Don't go nowhere."

Golden pulled his cap low over his brows and shoved his hands into the pockets of his hoodie as he strolled out of the room. He asked one of the nurses for directions to the ice machine, his mind still heavy with guilt. He walked right past the elevator lobby, completely missing Rich Loc stepping off, and heading in the opposite direction. Neither of them noticed each other, but fate was already at work.

Chapter 4

Rich Loc skidded to a stop outside the hospital, barely waiting for the car to come to a full halt before he jumped out and sprinted inside. His chest was tight, heart pounding, not from the run, but from the dread gripping him. He darted to the check-in desk; hands clenched.

"I need the room for Gabriella Milton," he demanded.

The clerk's fingers flew across the keyboard, eyes scanning the screen. She frowned. "I don't have that name on file. Are you sure?"

Rich Loc felt a sharp stab of frustration, his mind racing. Then, he remembered. "Aries," he muttered under his breath. "Look up Aries Wilkerson. She might be under that name."

The clerk checked again, and this time she nodded, printing a visitor's pass. "Room 523. Take the elevators to the fifth floor."

Rich Loc snatched the badge and slapped it onto his chest, already moving towards the elevator. He barely registered the hum of the hospital around him. His mind was focused on one thing, Aries. As he rode up, he tried to steady his breath, but his chest grew tighter. His brain was scrambled when the elevator doors opened, he had forgotten the room number.

He ran to the nurses' station. "Gabriella, I mean, Aries Wilkerson. What room is she in?" he asked, voice edged with impatience.

The nurse behind the counter glanced at him, then smiled a little too knowingly. "Second visitor in thirty minutes," she said. "Must be special, huh?"

Rich Loc's stomach dropped. "What do you mean, someone else was here?" His tone hardened. "Who was it? A man or a woman?"

"Guy," the nurse said casually. She gestured down the hall. "He went to get some ice. Oh, there he is."

Rich Loc turned, eyes narrowing as he spotted a man quickly ducking his head, trying to make a quiet exit toward the elevator. The guy dropped his cup of ice, shuffling faster. Rich Loc's blood ran cold when he recognized the face just before the elevator doors closed. Golden.

Without a second thought, Rich Loc bolted after him, adrenaline firing through his veins. He burst into the lobby just as the elevator closed. Golden's face lingered in his mind, calculating, hiding something.

For a second, Rich Loc stood there, fists clenching. He wanted to tear the doors open, drag Golden out, and settle whatever this was. But with Aries hurt, lying somewhere down the hall, he didn't have time to play games. Whatever Golden was up to, it could wait. Satisfied that he knew who it was, Rich Loc turned and made his way back toward the nurses' station.

The nurse was watching him. "Everything alright?" she asked, concerned.

Rich Loc forced himself to relax, masking the tension that rolled through him. "Yeah," he lied, voice calm. "Everything's smooth."

But nothing felt smooth. Something was off with Golden's presence. Rich Loc pushed the thought aside and focused on finding Aries. She needed him more than his feud with Golden did right now.

***

"Man, I think we shoulda tied this nigga up and stashed his ass in the hatch," Hush muttered, glancing back at Chris Stacks sprawled across the backseat, still out cold from the punch that had put him down.

"He good, son," Boodee replied, adjusting the rearview mirror with a steady hand. "The spot's 'bout what? Five, ten minutes? Duke ain't wakin' up."

"Nah, B, pull over into an alley or somethin'. I gotta bad feeling, yo."

Boodee rolled his eyes, a sigh escaping his lips. Hush had always been the paranoid one between them. "This nigga, man."

Hush lit the blunt they'd been passing since they left the hospital, blowing out a thick cloud of smoke that filled the truck. Boodee coughed, waving the smoke away, his eyes scanning for a safe spot to pull over.

"You seriously need to fall back on the chiefin', bro," Boodee complained, his voice tense. "I'm tellin' you, it's makin' you paranoid. Ain't no way in hell this pork belly, rump roast muthafucka gon' wake—"

Boodee screamed loud enough for God and all the angels in heaven to hear him when Chris popped up and sunk his teeth into the soft flesh of his cheek. Growling, he bit into him like he was a ripe, juicy apple, and pulled away, taking a chunk of meat with him.

"Get 'em, son. Get this muthafucka off me." Boodee hollered, swerving the truck this way and that way, trying to fight Chris off.

The blunt fell onto Hush's lap. He rose up from the passenger seat, smacking it off before it could burn through his jeans. That's when he heard a scream that felt like it would burst his left eardrum. He looked at Boodee and he was in tears, awkwardly punching Chris in the side of his face. Chris had latched onto Boodee's ear, growling again, shaking his head like an angry pit-bull. Blood streamed down the side of Boodee's face but he kept punching Chris.

By this time, Hush was giving him Haymakers to the back of his head, but no matter how hard he struck him, it didn't seem to faze him.

"Get off of 'em. Get the fuck off my mans," Hush spat furiously, punching him with all his might.

"Shoot 'em, Hush. Shoot this fat muthafuckaaaa," Boodee cried. His voice went up a couple of octaves as Chris abruptly snatched back, taking Boodee's ear.

Chris spat out the severed ear. There was so much blood around his mouth he looked like a goddamn vampire.

"Fuck that, son. I'm 'bouta pop this nigga," Hush declared, activating the stashbox to retrieve his gun.

"Oh shit." Boodee's eyes lit up as a big-ass Mack truck flew at them full speed ahead.

Hush threw up his leg and both hands. Screaming for his life, he turned his head, not wanting to see what was coming next. The Mack truck's driver honked his horn three times. Then he laid on it, producing an annoying sound.

At the last minute, Boodee managed to swerve out of its path, but the side view mirror of his Chevy Suburban got knocked off. His truck was fish-tailed, but he was able to regain control and mash its brake pedal. The vehicle jerked to a halt.

"Learn how to drive before you fuckin' kill someone, asshole," the Mack truck driver shouted out of his window, throwing up the "fuck you" finger. Hush and Boodee's hearts thudded as they tried to catch their breath, thankful to still be among the living. Hush crossed himself in the crucifix sign and kissed his fingers up to God. Boodee winced in pain as he bled, looking like some shit out of a Clive Barker novel.

Suddenly, the back door flew open. Chris Stacks, barefoot and wearing nothing but his blood-stained hospital gown, jumped out on the pavement and took off running, his butt cheeks jiggling in the moonlight.

"We gotta get this muthafucka," Hush said, with urgency in his voice. He removed two guns from the stash box and passed one to Boodee.

They jumped out of the truck, adrenaline pumping, and chased Chris down the dark, alleyway, their sticks cocked and ready for whatever.

Hush and Boodee's foreheads wrinkled with confusion when they reached the end of the alleyway and Chris was gone. It was like he vanished into thin air, on some Houdini-type shit.

"Where the fuck this nigga go?" Hush muttered, his voice dripping irritation.

"I don't know," Boodee replied, scanning their surroundings carefully. "Maybe he dipped into one of these backyards."

Hush raised his brows as he looked at him skeptically. "Man, hell nah. Not that fast. His chunky ass probably hidin' in some of this garbage around here. Come on." He nudged Boodee to follow as he crept forward, his eyes darting around the alleyway's dark recesses. "Remember, Boo, don't pop this nigga to kill 'em. Shoot below the waist. Wood wants 'em back alive so he can get Rich Loc."

Boodee nodded. "Understood. But once we're done with his mans, I'm slicin' off some premium cuts of meats for what he did to my fuckin' face."

"I ain't mad at chu, Boo. I'd be tryna catch my issue, too."

The alleyway was strangely quiet, except for the distant barking of dogs and the occasional car passing by. They moved slowly, carefully picking through old furniture and garbage, their senses sharp and on high alert.

Suddenly, Chris Stacks lunged out from behind a pile of junk with a big ass 4x4. Hearing the rustling behind him, Boodee swung around just in time to see the attack coming. He raised his gun, but Chris swung with all his might, knocking the gun out of his hand as it discharged, sending the bullet whizzing harmlessly into the night. Chris followed up with a powerful kick to Boodee's chest, sending him flying back into a mound of lumpy garbage bags.

Hush aimed for Chris's thigh, but Chris hurled the 4x4 at him like it was a harpoon, forcing Hush to duck as it smashed into the wall behind him. Chris closed the gap instantly, tackling Hush into an old, rusted refrigerator, and raining fists down on him. Hush barely had time to shield himself from the relentless assault.

Boodee, still recovering, saw a window of opportunity he couldn't afford to let close. He scooped up the 4x4 Chris hurled at Hush and crept up behind him. He swung it across the back of Chris's skull. And the impact sounded like a bat connecting with a baseball. Chris fell on top of Hush, knocked out cold and snoring.

"Man, help get this nigga off me."

Boodee strained as he struggled to push Chris's dead weight off Hush.

Hush staggered up, shaking his head to clear the daze and dusting himself off. He suddenly stopped when his eyes locked on Chris. His anger bubbled over and he kicked Chris in his side. "That's for givin' us all this trouble kidnappin' yo' ass."

Boodee, wanting to get a piece of the action, followed up with a vicious kick of his own. "And that's for my face and my ear," he snarled, spitting on the unconscious man for good measure.

Hush and Boodee got right to work gagging and tying Chris up, making sure the knots were tight. This time, they weren't taking any chances. They hoisted his limp body and stuffed him into the hatch.

"See you inna minute Criss Angel," Hush said, slamming the hatch shut with a sense of finality.

***

Golden, fury coursing through his veins, paced the elevator like a caged animal. His breathing was erratic, and his fists trembled with anger and frustration. "Fuck this," he muttered under his breath and punched the elevator wall. "Ducking from this gump-ass nigga like I owe 'em money or something. Nah, not me. Not no more."

He pulled the shoestring from his Timb, wrapped it tightly around his fists, and pulled it taut. It was thin but strong enough to do what he needed. He coiled and uncoiled it, thinking about how easy it would be to sneak up behind Rich Loc and end everything there. Just one move, quick and silent.

The elevator dinged, and Golden stepped out into the lobby. But as he waited for the next elevator to take him back up, something shifted inside him. His heartbeat, pounding moments earlier with rage, began to slow, the fire in his chest dimming. He stood there, the shoestring clutched in his hands, and a thought crept in. *This is reckless. This is prison time.* He had too much to lose.

Golden let out a long, steady breath, his hands slowly relaxing. The shoestring fell limp between his fingers. He slipped it back into his pocket, his body still humming with tension, but his mind clearing. No. He wasn't going to let his emotions drive him into something he couldn't take back.

With a final glance back at the elevator, Golden walked out of the hospital. His mind spun. He was torn between wanting revenge and realizing this wasn't the way. Not yet.

Chapter 5

"What the fuck happened to yo' face?" Wood frowned, noticing the dressing on Boodee's cheek. His eyes narrowed when he saw his mangled ear. "Goddamn, Boo, looks like a grizzly got ahold of you."

"You're right. And the animal that attacked 'em is sitting right there," Hush chimed in, nodding toward Chris.

Wood looked at Chris like he was a beast at the Zoo. "If the nigga was hungry, y'all shoulda bought 'em something to eat." He patted Boodee on his shoulder, rubbing the side of his head. "You're gonna be a'ight. I'ma get the doc to take a look at chu, make sho' that wound doesn't get infected a'ight?"

Boodee nodded.

"Good, boy." He turned to Hush. "Yo, get our boy onna jack and see how soon he can check out Boodee." With that, Wood set his sights on Chris. He approached him, grabbing a chair along the way. He planted the chair backward before Chris and sat down on it. "You know that's really fucked up how you done my man, Boo. Those wounds are gonna cost me a hell of a lotta bread in plastic surgery. I guess that's the cost of being the boss, huh?" He snorted, pulling on his nose. He'd taken a couple of bumps of coke before he'd dropped by. The evidence was reflected in his drowsy eyes. "A'ight let's get down to business. You're here on account of ya boy, Big Rich. Yo' big bro. Ya brother had some of his guys take my God brother, Trell, may he rest in peace, off the shelf.

His death left me and my family, especially his father, my godfather, with bleeding hearts. So, it's only right that blood answers for blood. Luckily for you, I want yo' brother in exchange for you. If he agrees to deliver himself to me, on my soul, I'll uncuff you from that pole and escort chu outta here myself. Deal?"

Wood watched as Chris leaned against the pole, mind racing. He didn't wanna die and he didn't want his brother getting acquainted with dude's machete. Making up his mind, he nodded in agreement, taking a deep breath.

"Okay. Do you know yo' brother's number by heart?"

Chris nodded.

"A'ight. You've got a number and I've got a phone," he removed his cellphone from his pocket, flashing it at Chris. He asked for Rich Loc's telephone number. Listening to the phone ring, Wood pulled a bandana up over his nose and signaled for Hush and Boo to do the same.

Rich Loc picked up on the fourth ring. "Who this?"

"Mr. Rich Loc," Wood answered with a tinge of hostility. "I have yo' lil' bro in front of me. And if you want 'em back, I want chu in exchange. You come alone, if not I'ma—"

"Wait. Wait. Wait." Rich Loc perked up. "What the fuck is goin on? What's this about?"

"This is about you sending yo goons to jack my spot and leaving my family dead," Wood growled into the receiver. He was on his feet now, pacing, Hush and Boodee watching him in the background. "Over territory that's not even yours. Don't play stupid with me, dick." He kicked the chair he was seated in across the room. He was furious now, clenching his cellphone so tight his knuckles cracked.

"My nigga, I didn't have anyone knocked down over—" Rich Loc was cut short by Chris's pain-filled screams as Wood sliced his arm, spilling his blood.

"You hear that, drug lord? Shit just got real. Get it together and hit me back. You've got four minutes." Wood hung up. Head down, holding his cellphone at his back, he started pacing the floor again.

His breath came in sharp, controlled bursts as he ran a hand over his 360-waves, eyes darting to the blood-forming around Chris's arm. Hush and Boodee shifted uneasily, but neither dared to speak. The tension in the room crackled like live wires.

Wood stopped pacing and turned back toward Chris, still slumped against the pole, a dark stain spreading across his shirt where the blood flowed freely from his wound. Chris's face was pale, his breaths shallow, but he gritted his teeth and forced himself not to cry out again. He wasn't going to give Wood the satisfaction.

Wood knelt, his voice dropping to a whisper, cold as ice. "Listen, kid," he muttered, his eyes boring into Chris's. "I don't want to hurt you more than I have to, but you and your brother got my people twisted in knots. You think you can make this right; you better pray he calls back. 'Cause if he don't…"

His voice trailed off; the silence more menacing than his threats. Chris swallowed hard, his mind racing, trying to come up with any plan, any angle that might get him out of this alive. He glanced at Hush and Boodee, gauging their expressions. Boodee was still fuming, eyes locked on him like a predator ready to pounce. Hush seemed more aloof, but his eyes betrayed a curiosity, as if he were waiting to see what would happen next.

***

After Wood hung up with his ultimatum, Rich Loc looked at Angel as she lay asleep in bed. Rising from his chair, he approached the large window that gave a stunning view of the city at night. He'd done a lot of dirt, and he ordered a lot of dirt to be done. But he was 100% sure he didn't have anyone executed over drug territory. He only dealt in weight.

He couldn't explain that to Wood. He already had his mind made up and wanted his life for some shit he didn't do. His back was against the wall. The pressure on him was immense. But he didn't have to think twice about the decision. If walking inside the lions' den meant his brother would live to see another sunrise, then he'd walk in that bitch naked, drenched in blood.

Rich Loc glanced at his timepiece. He had one minute left to tell Wood what he was going to do before he chopped Chris into sushi. With a deep breath, he hit Wood back up as he walked inside the restroom, locking the door behind him.

"A'ight, you want me, then you got me," Rich Loc said, once Wood answered. "But first, I wanna know fa sho' that that's really my brother you got. I wanna see his face, hear his voice at the very least." *If this nigga really does have bro, how did he get 'em? He was laid up in the hospital not long ago*, he thought.

"I'll hit chu back inna sec," Wood told him.

"Bet." Rich Loc disconnected the call. He got a call from the hospital Chris Stacks was admitted to. He hoped Wood was bluffing about having Chris, and this was his doctor trying to update him on his condition.

"What's up? This is he." A frown slowly emerged on his face. "What the fuck do you mean is he with me? Y'all supposed to have 'em. Ain't this 'bouta bitch." He ran his hand down his face and listened to what he was being told. His heart was beating like a tribal drum on the sands of Samoa. Niggaz really did have Chris held captive. "Yo, I don't have no time for this shit, cuz. Y'all better find my br—"

Rich Loc was cut short by a Facetime call from Wood. He hung up on the doctor and picked right up. His stomach twisted in knots and he felt sick when he saw Chris handcuffed to a pole and saturated in blood.

"That's him. That's baby bro," Wood said from behind the cellphone. "Now you know it's not a game over here. So are you coming, or what? Let a nigga know."

"Fuck these niggaz, bro. You know how we get down," Chris roared, eyes angry and pink. "It's me and you, from the womb to the tomb, baby. From the womb to the to—"

A kick to the grill silenced Chris, and the call was disconnected. Wood disconnected the call, leaving Rich Loc wondering what fate would fall upon his brother. Tears slowly accumulated in his eyes and spilled down his cheeks. Sniffling, he wiped them away and walked out of the restroom. As the door clicked closed behind him, he dropped down on his hands and knees, weakened by yet another death of someone he loved.

"My man, I thought we had an understanding," Wood shook his head like he couldn't believe how incredibly stupid Chris was. "You just took yo' destiny into your own hands. Y'all tighten this nigga up." He snapped his fingers, signaling Hush and Boodee to carry out his command.

They punched and kicked Chris until their arms and legs were tired. Chris's face was swollen, his nose was at an impossible angle, and his right eye had balled shut. Wheezing like he was trying to blow a broken whistle, Chris spat blood and licked his swollen lips. Wood, LaCresha at his side, stood at the center of Hush and Boodee. They were staring at him like they were trying to figure out what to do to him next.

Wood flipped his machete over in his gloved hand and passed it to Boodee by its blade. "Give homie the proper send-off, kid, and bathe my lady once you finish." Wood patted Boodee on his shoulder as he turned around, walking away. Once the door clicked shut behind Boodee, he admired LaCresha like she was the most beautiful woman in the world. He looked upon her in admiration, swinging and thrusting her, imagining the damage she could do when in contact with human flesh.

Standing on the sideline, Hush pulled his bandana around his neck and folded his arms across his chest. He watched as

Boodee approached him with a creepy smile, and eyes lusting for blood.

"Yeaaah, it's just you, me, and this pretty lil' bitch right here," Boodee spoke of the machete clenched in his fist. He stood in front of Chris, his shadow looming over him. He found it peculiar that Chris was looking past him.

Boodee's eyebrows creased as he wondered what had his attention. He glanced back but he didn't see anyone. When he looked back at Chris, he was wearing a grin on his lips and tears were dancing in his eyes. Hush took note of his staring at something other than Boodee, too. He looked around the room, but there wasn't anyone present besides the three of them. Not knowing what to make of it, he shrugged and focused back on the show.

A blurred image of Jamaica, Chris's wifey, who'd been killed during the home invasion and robbery, advanced in his direction.

"Long time, no see, hubs," Jamaica smiled, displaying the small gap between her teeth. "I've missed you."

"I've missed you, too," Chris replied, tears streaking his cheeks. "I love you."

Boodee looked around confused. He didn't know what the hell was Chris's trip, but it had him weirded out. He looked at Hush and shrugged like *I don't know what's up with this nigga.*

"I love you, too, baby. You ready to go home?" Jamaica asked, walking past Hush, with no acknowledgment from him.

Chris slightly nodded and whispered, "Yeah."

LaCresha made a sickening sound as she broke through the surface of Chris's scalp, piercing his skull, and embedding inside his brain. His eyes crossed as blood poured out of his wound, running down his face. Boodee pressed his sneaker against Chris's chest, pinning him against the pole. With three strong tugs, he retrieved the machete, but kept his sneaker planted on Chris's chest.

Grunting, he swung the blade sideways into the side of his neck. Boodee closed his eyes momentarily as blood splattered on his face. Breathing hard, he continued his barbaric assault until he felt better about the damage done to his face.

"You feel better now?" Hush asked.

Boodee wiped the blood from his face and looked back at Hush. "Definitely. That was, uh, that was very therapeutic."

Sighing, Hush shook his head. "You needa see a shrink, you know that?"

"Whatever, man. Get fat boy ready for the big chop, while I give LaCresha a bath."

Boodee walked away, looking the machete over like she was someone special in his life.

Chapter 6

Six Black and Puerto Rican kids battled it out on a sun-faded basketball court in the neighborhood park. Their game was a chaotic symphony of sneakers screeching against cracked pavement and shouts bouncing off graffiti-stained walls. The ball whipped around like it was on fire, every kid trying to be the hero of the play. Sweat dripped down their faces, blending with the dust and grit of the court. Suddenly, the ball found its way to an open player near the three-point line. His defender, caught off-guard while trying to double-team someone else, spun around too late. The kid with the ball squared up, launched a deep shot and held his breath as the ball soared through the air.

Clang.

The shot rattled off the rim, sailed over the rusty chain-link fence, and landed with a hollow thud on the other side. It bounced lazily across the street, rolling to a stop near a pile of garbage bags, slumped against the curb.

"I got it," Gino, one of the Puerto Rican kids, shouted. He was quick on his feet, scaling the fence in one swift move. He hit the pavement on the other side, knees bending to absorb the impact, then jogged across the street, glancing both ways for traffic. He reached down, snatched up the ball, and was about to head back when something in one of the trash bags caught his attention. A dark, wet shine glimmered through the torn plastic, a glint that didn't belong.

Curiosity nagged at him. He pushed the ball under his arm and leaned closer, peeling back the ripped edge of the garbage bag. The stench hit him first, sharp and sickly sweet, like something rotting in the sun. His eyes widened as he took in the contents—a slick, horrifying mess of flesh and bone. His stomach lurched, and before he knew it, he was throwing up pinkish-green bile, his insides heaving as he stumbled back.

"Gino, what's up? What happened?" one of the kids yelled, seeing his friend bent over, retching like his guts were being ripped out.

The others, sensing something was wrong, climbed over the fence and sprinted to his side. They gathered around Gino, each one craning their neck to see what had him so messed up. As they peered into the bag, the horror of what they were looking at hit them like a dump truck. Chris Stacks' severed head stared up at them, eyes half-closed in a twisted, empty gaze that seemed to follow them no matter where they moved. Blood-matted hair clung to the skull, while the rest of his dismembered body parts, arms, legs, and hands still clutching at nothing, were crammed into the bag like discarded trash.

***

Remo sat back on his aunt's couch, sharing a blunt with his little cousin Lou, half listening to him bitch and complain about his gig at Burger King. He'd gotten laid off a few hours ago for short-changing the register. Now he was trying to convince Remo to give him a seat at his table. This wasn't the first time the young nigga had tried to put an application in with him. Although Remo admired his consistency, his cousin had become annoying as fuck. He started to brush him off, but he didn't have it in him to hurt his feelings. He knew he'd looked up to him since he was knee-high, and practically did any and everything he asked of him. So, he thought maybe it wouldn't be so bad to try him out to see what kind of asset he'd be to the team.

"I'm sayin' cuzzo, I know you've been puttin' together a crew," Lou continued, passing the blunt back to Remo and releasing smoke from his nose. "And who better to watch yo' back than yo' blood? You know yo' fam ain't scared to put no work in."

Remo nodded as he continued listening to Lou. He pulled out his cellphone and hit up his connect. He was on the phone all of three minutes when he hung up with an agreement to link up for some work.

"So, how 'bout it, cousin? You gon' put yo' family down or what?" Lou looked at Remo with hopeful eyes. Remo couldn't help thinking how much he looked like his younger self asking to be taken to the corner bodega.

Remo blew smoke from his nostril as he leaned forward, smashing out what was left of his blunt. "You know how to work a pump action shotgun?"

Lou smiled like he'd been waiting his whole life for this moment.

***

Rich Loc hung up with Parelli, after instructing him to get four birds from the stash spot to deliver to Remo. He wasn't foolish enough to tell him outright over the jack what he wanted him to do. For all he knew, the Alphabet Boys had his shit tapped. That was why he and Parelli had a way of talking to each other when it came to business. If anyone were listening, they'd think Rich Loc was telling Parelli to grab a few containers of chocolate frosting for a cake he was baking. They'd been moving like this for years and getting away with it.

Rich Loc disconnected the call and slipped his cellphone inside his pocket. He posted up at the back of the room, allowing his family to say their final goodbyes to his brother's closed casket. For as long as he and Chris Stacks had been little niggaz running the streets, chasing ass, getting money, and getting into trouble, he never stopped to think the day would come for one of them to be inside of one of these places. Even with the number of niggas they'd dealt this same fate to, he never thought about the time coming when it was their time to pay the piper.

Rich Loc kissed and hugged his aunts and embraced the men of his family as they headed out the door. He requested that the funeral home director give him a minute alone with his brother before he closed shop. The director nodded, closing the double wooden doors behind him as he left.

With a heavy heart, Rich Loc walked down the aisle, trying to think of what his last words would be to his brother.

"Man, bro, if you would have told me this day was coming, I wouldn't have believed you," Rich Loc said, batting away his tears. "You and me, we had a whole lotta mo' living between us. We were 'pose to go out as old niggaz, babysitting our grandkids while our sons and daughters ran the streets, tearing shit up like we used to." Feeling like he was going to breakdown, he took the time to gather himself and cleared his throat. "I want chu to know this isn't goodbye. It's more like I'll see you later. I paid these people good money to speed up yo' wake and cremate chu. I'll be back to pick you up in a few days. I love you, bro." He kissed his forehead and walked towards the doors.

Rich Loc's cellphone rang with a call from Detective Rollins. He blew an annoyed breath, knowing what he wanted, but answered anyway.

***

Detective Rollins had become a real pain in Rich Loc's ass, hounding him nonstop for the past few days about the brick he was supposed to deliver. Rich Loc, fucked up over Aries getting shot and Chris Stacks being brutally butchered, had been sending Rollins' calls straight to voicemail. But when the detective threatened to plant enough dope on him to land a sentence that'd look like a phone number, Rich Loc knew he had to make the drop asap.

Rollins paced the kitchen floor like a man on the edge. Every few minutes, he'd unlock the back door and peek outside, searching for Rich Loc's car by the backyard gate. The anticipation had him antsy, jittery, desperate. He was so deep in his addiction that he had spent the better part of an hour on his knees in the living room, combing through the carpet for anything that resembled crack to smoke. Coming up empty-handed only fueled his frustration and further pissed him off.

Hearing someone knock at the front door caused his nerves to shoot up a notch. His brows wrinkled as he wondered who it could have been. He wasn't expecting anyone besides Rich Loc, and they agreed he'd entered through the backdoor. He stashed the items he'd need to cook the coke under the kitchen sink, pocketed his crack pipe and lighter, and approached the door cautiously, keeping his hand near his stick.

When Rollins pulled back the curtain, he was surprised to see Rich Loc standing on his porch. He quickly let him in and stuck his head outside to make sure no one saw him enter. Locking the door behind him, he turned and led Rich Loc into the kitchen, like an overbearing parent ready to scold a rebellious teenager.

"Dude, I told you to come through the back," Rollins snapped, his voice edged with panic. "I got the nosiest fuckin' neighbors on the planet. You know how it'll look if they see you here? You're a fuckin' drug dealer, for Christ's sake."

And you're a fucking crackhead, Rich Loc thought, rolling his eyes. He was barely able to suppress his annoyance. He had bigger problems to deal with, and hearing Rollins' whining wasn't making any of it better. He watched as the detective ducked under the sink to pull out the ingredients to cook up the coke, all while muttering under his breath.

"You hear me talkin' to you?" Rollins barked, straightening up and placing the baking soda on the table.

"Yeah, man, I hear you," Rich Loc muttered, extending the shopping bag with the bird inside. "Look, I gotta go, so here."

But Rollins wasn't having it. Face twisted into a scowl, he stepped into Rich Loc's personal space, his stale breath invading the air between them.

"Nah, I needa hear you say it," Rollins growled, leaning in even closer. "Say it. Say, 'I hear you, Massa Rollins.'"

Rich Loc froze and glared at him in disbelief. "Yo, son, I don't know what the fuck's gotten into you, but I'm not in the mood for your lil' games."

"I'm not gonna tell you again, nigger."

Rich Loc's blood ran hot, and rage boiled inside him. Before he even knew what he was doing, his hand was already reaching for the piece tucked in his waistband. Rollins saw the move and went for his own holstered pistol, but he was slow, too slow.

Poc.

The first shot ripped through Rollins' chest. His eyes went wide in shock as a dark red spot expanded on his shirt. He stumbled but tried to reach for his gun again. Rich Loc didn't give him the chance.

Poc. Poc. Poc.

The shots rang out, each one hitting its mark as Rollins staggered, his body moving as if underwater. He lunged forward, arms flailing, trying to grab Rich Loc in a desperate bear hug, but Rich Loc was already stepping back, letting his gun do the talking.

Rollins crashed into the kitchen table, toppling over it and landing flat on his back. His eyes, once filled with arrogance and superiority, now stared lifelessly up at the ceiling. His mouth hung open, as if frozen in mid-sentence.

Rich Loc stepped forward, standing over his body, his lip curled in disgust. "Cracka-ass muthafucka," he snarled, biting down on his lip. "You thought you could come at me like I'm some kinda field nigga? You got me fucked up, cuz."

With one final burst of rage, he fired three more shots into Rollins' chest. Empty shell casings clattered to the floor and rolled to a stop near the detective's blood-soaked body. Rich Loc looked down at him, breathing heavily, heart pounding.

He dropped the shopping bag next to Rollins' still form. "There's yo' brick, bitch."

Rich Loc slipped out the back door and disappeared into the night.

Chapter 7

A couple of nights ago, Golden returned from New York, to find Cowboy sitting quietly in the dark on the couch. Golden apologized a thousand times for chaining him up like a dog. Cowboy's expression remained stoic. He didn't say shit.

"Look, Cow, I wanna letchu outta here, but I needa know that you're okay," Golden said, kneeling before Cowboy. "You haven't been seeing yo' moms, or thangs that really aren't there. Have you? Keep it a buck with me, big bruh."

Cowboy, wearing an unreadable look, looked him in the eyes. "I'm fucked up, lil' bruh. I need help. I mean I really, really need help. I see why you chained me here." He held up his shackled wrist. "I could fuck around and do something to myself, or you." his voice cracked with emotion and his eyes turned glassy. He was on the verge of tears. "I'm not gon' front on you, G. I have been seeing my moms and some more shit. But I've been fighting, and fighting, and fighting to maintain control."

"Come here, man," Golden gave him a brotherly hug. "I gotchu, bruh. I gotchu. Whatever demons you're fighting, I'ma fight 'em witchu. We're brothers, for life."

"For life," Cowboy said in agreeance.

"You think you'll be straight 'til Monday? I can make a few calls then and see about you seeing someone. If you can't see anyone ASAP, then we'll just kick it in the emergency ward and see what they can do for you." He gripped his

shoulder, showing emotional support, watching tears roll down his cheeks.

Cowboy nodded as he wiped the wetness from his eyes. "I got this. I can hold it down until Monday."

"You sho'?" Golden took a closer look, searching for any hesitance in his face. He didn't see any.

"I'ma hun-do, bro." He nodded with assurance.

"A'ight," Golden said, withdrawing the key to the shackle from his pocket.

As soon as he unlocked it, Cowboy rubbed his sore wrist, and Golden pulled him up on his feet. Abruptly, Cowboy hugged him like he hadn't seen him in years. He cried like a big baby. Golden did too. "Come on. I'ma draw you a bath 'cause yo' ass hummin'," he smiled.

"Man, fuck you," Cowboy threw his arm around his shoulders, kissing his cheek as they walked down the hallway. "I love you."

"I love you, too, big bruh."

***

Golden moved around the kitchen like a contestant on *Chopped*, preparing a dinner that consisted of smothered pork chops, mac & cheese, mustard greens, candy yams, and cornbread.

One would think Shirvetta was the one who had taught her children how to cook, but they had Heavy to thank for that. He knew his way around the kitchen better than most housewives. Most times, he cooked dinner for the family. The twins and the boys liked it that way. Shirvetta could burn, but she didn't have shit on Heavy.

Golden turned the fire off the greens and removed a pan of cornbread from the oven. Closing his eyes, he inhaled the aroma wafting from its surface and a grin tugged at the corner of his lips. Turning off the oven, he set the pan on the stove and made two plates. He placed them on the table, removed his apron, and hung it on the back of the kitchen door.

Golden pulled out his cellphone and called the hospital for an update on Aries's condition. As he knocked on Cowboy's door to tell him dinner was ready, one of the nurses picked up.

"Hey. How are you? I'm good. And yourself," Golden said into the phone. "Smooth. I was calling to get an update on Aries Wilkerson." As he listened to what he was being told, the jovial expression fell from Golden's face and Cowboy opened the door.

"What's up, G?" Cowboy's brows wrinkled, seeing Golden teary-eyed.

"D—dinners ready," Golden said, tears sliding down his cheeks. "Okay, uh, um, thank you." He disconnected the call and slid the cellphone into his pocket.

Worry etched into Cowboy's features as he grasped Golden's shoulders. "Golden, what's good?"

Golden closed his eyes momentarily and cleared his throat before speaking. He had a devastated look on his face. "It's Aries. She, uh, she…she didn't make it."

Something inside Cowboy snapped, and with a guttural growl, he exploded, attacking Golden with terrifying fury. He threw fists, elbows, knees, and kicks against Golden's head and body, treating him like a Wing Chun fight dummy.

The force of Cowboy's assault left Golden stunned and barely able to react. It was like trying to fight off a wild animal. Cowboy seemed possessed by a supernatural force.

Cowboy overpowered Golden with raw, savage strength. Each blow felt like it was driving deeper into his core, knocking the air from his lungs and rattling his bones. Cowboy slammed Golden into either wall of the hallway, bloodying his nose and busting his mouth. Golden hit the floor with a thud, battered and bruised.

Cowboy's eyes were ablaze as he stood over him, breathing heavily. He raised his foot, ready to crush his skull and finish it. Golden, dazed and barely holding on to consciousness, could only watch through swollen eyes.

"Cowboy, I'm, I'm yo' brother, man. It's, it's me, Go—Golden," Golden said weakly.

No, mommy. Leave 'em alone. As far as I'm concerned, Golden's the only brother I got left, he tried to help me, Cowboy thought, taking full control of his body.

Right then, something changed in Cowboy, his face softened, and the rage disappeared, just as fast as it came. He lowered his foot. It wasn't Cowboy standing there anymore. It was Chick.

Sweat slid down Cowboy's face as he stepped back, trembling. He had taken over completely, shutting down the madness that nearly made Chick kill his brother.

Without saying a word, Cowboy ran to the bedroom and frantically pulled clothes from the dresser, throwing them on. Mind racing, he slipped into his jeans and his leather boots with the spurs.

He looked back at Golden one last time. He wasn't moving, and he could barely hear him breathing. But he didn't have time for guilt, not now.

Cowboy snatched the front door open and took a deep breath of the night air. The cool breeze hit his face, but he didn't look back again. Without hesitation, he closed the door behind himself and disappeared into the darkness.

***

Blinking into consciousness, Golden discovered his head throbbing and his ears ringing. With a groan, he peeled himself off the floor, the soreness of his body screaming at him, with every movement. Something told him to check his cellphone. He took it from his pocket and its screen was cracked. He checked his latest voice message. Remo had called him ten minutes ago. He dropped the location to

Parelli's work and the address where he was meeting Rich Loc.

"My location to my iPhone is on, my nigga. If you don't hear from me in a dub, track me down, and bust in, making everythang dead that ain't me. Gone."

Golden slipped the cellphone back into his pocket. Then a name struck him like a bolt of lightning from the heavens.

Cowboy!

The thought of his older brother snapped Golden fully awake, and his pulse quickened. Panic spread like the Black Plague as flashes of last night's brawl flooded his mind. As long as they'd been alive, he'd never seen such rage in Cowboy's eyes. He'd thrown Golden around like he was a rag doll. He was on the verge of killing him, and then, he just stopped.

Golden snatched his gun off the floor, where it had fallen, and got to his feet. He moved through the house like he was on fire, snatching open doors and shouting Cowboy's name into every empty room.

Nothing.

His stomach sank. *Where the fuck is he?*

He rushed to the garage and his worst fear was confirmed—Heavy's old ride was gone. The only thing that remained were the oil stains on the ground where the car had been parked.

Golden slammed his fist into the garage wall, but the sharp pain in his knuckles barely registered over the fear twisting in his gut. Car keys in hand, he ran back to the front of the house.

He most likely went back home. I can probably catch up with 'em.

Golden stepped foot in the driveway and disappointment hit him like the open hand of a scorned girlfriend. His ride was still there, but all of its tires were flat.

"Fuck!" Golden roared, kicking the passenger door so hard the metal buckled. His chest heaved as he balled his fists so tight his knuckles bulged. He was as hot as lava.

He kicked the door harder this time, leaving an even larger dent. He needed to get back to New York. Every second counted. If he didn't catch up to Cowboy soon, he'd wind up dead or behind bars. Pulling out his cellphone, Golden ordered a Triple-A plan and arranged for someone to meet him with a new set of tires.

***

As Cowboy stepped into his basement apartment, his eyes narrowed at the chaos unfolding before him. His neighbors were tearing through his belongings like vultures, rummaging for anything valuable he may have to steal. They were so caught up in their frantic search that they didn't even notice he had arrived.

Cowboy let out a low whistle. The sound sliced through the air, stopping the intruders dead in their tracks. Startled, they spun around to face him, their expressions shifting from arrogance to fear when they saw who stood before them.

"Well, well, look who decided to show up," one of them sneered, voice trembling slightly.

Cowboy remained silent, his gaze cold and unforgiving. Slowly, with a firm grip, he raised his shotgun. The tension in the room thickened as the neighbors began to realize just how badly they had fucked up.

"You shouldn't have come here," Cowboy finally spoke, his voice a low, threatening rumble. "This is my crib. You crossed the line."

Before any of them could react, the roar of his shotgun filled the space, and a deafening blast reverberated off the walls. The intruders crumpled to the floor, their bodies twisted and lifeless, their screams cut short by the brutal force of the shot.

Cowboy lowered his weapon and turned his attention to the makeshift brick wall where he'd hidden his stash. With quick, determined movements, he pried the bricks loose, revealing a cache of money. A smirk crept onto his face. "Just what I was looking for."

He swiftly loaded the bundles of cash into duffle bags, feeling the weight of his sins bear down on him with each handful. "Time to get outta this hellhole," he muttered.

But he wasn't leaving just yet. Shrugging into his weathered duster coat, the leather creaking softly against his broad shoulders, Cowboy reached for his Colt Peacemakers, the heavy revolvers settling comfortably in his hands like old friends.

Stepping out, Cowboy knew he was walking straight into trouble. But with his guns at his side, he was ready for whatever lay ahead.

Chapter 8

Cowboy started up the car and glanced in the rearview mirror. His mother was in the back seat, lighting up a cigarette. She exhaled a cloud of smoke and eyed the square like it was an old lover.

"Been a long time since I had one of these," Chick said, taking another drag from her Newport.

"Ma, I don't know how I let you talk me into this," Cowboy muttered, shaking his head. "I must be outta my damn mind."

"If you wanna make things right with the Big Man, you gotta put some good back in the world, son." She took a long pull on her cigarette and looked at him with serious eyes. "I've been watchin' you, junior. Seen every move you made since I've been gone. And lemme tell you, the bad outweighs the good. We gotta balance them books, if you ever wanna be in the Big Man's good graces."

Cowboy sighed, exasperated. "Alright, Ma, I'll do it, but only 'cause it's you."

Chick smiled, her face softening. "Thank you, baby," she whispered, leaning forward to kiss his cheek. "If this is so hard for you, why don't I take over from here?"

Cowboy yawned, exhaustion pulling at him. "I am kinda tired."

"So how about it, baby boy?" Chick's smile widened.

"Okay, Ma."

"Ooooh, thank you, sonshine," she cooed, hugging him from behind, and planting a kiss on his cheek. Cowboy felt his cheeks warm under his mother's affection.

She nodded toward the curb. "Pull over here."

Cowboy did as she instructed, then slumped back in his seat and closed his eyes. As sleep crept over him, he was suddenly jolted awake, only to find himself in his mother's body. Chick grinned at her reflection in the sun visor, blowing a kiss to her image. With a flick, she shut the visor and slid on a pair of black sunglasses.

She turned the radio dial, frowning at the modern music blaring from the speakers. Then she perked up as "Flashlight" came on, bobbing her head and singing along. "This used to be my jam," she murmured, merging smoothly into traffic.

Chick, carrying a heavy sack over her shoulder like Santa Claus, walked the streets of Brooklyn, leaving racks of cash in mailboxes and tossing them on porches like the morning paper. She wandered through the projects, knocking on doors and handing out racks to everyone in sight, crackheads, homeless people, kids, elders, mothers, fathers, anyone who was a part of the black community. As she moved, the neighborhood erupted in joy, and Chick, happy, threw bills from the car window like rice at a wedding.

***

"You think he'll be inside?" Chick asked Cowboy, eyeing the familiar house from the driver's seat.

"Yeah, Ma," Cowboy replied. "Knowing that lil' nigga, he's definitely in there. See his bike over there?" He nodded toward a Huffy bicycle leaned against the side of the house.

"Alright, let's go say hi," Chick said, adjusting the revolvers in their holsters before sliding out of the car.

***

Cordare and his crew were busy cooking drugs, intermittently glancing at a boxing match on the TV. Each had a job, and Reese, a young nigga Cowboy had shot on a previous raid, was tasked with bagging the drugs. The bullet wound had left Reese with a shit bag, but it hadn't driven him from the streets. Instead, it made him go harder. He had to keep hustling to support his family. Flipping burgers and mopping floors wasn't going to pay the bills, so he stuck with what would.

"Damn, he's got hands," Reese said, his attention bouncing between his work and the fight.

"Yo, you see how son moves? He's quick with it," Cordare added from behind a bandana, stirring a Pyrex pot with a box of baking soda in hand. "Nigga got reflexes like Spider-Man."

The whole crew was mesmerized by the match, but then…

Spiiiinn. Click. Spiiiinn. Click. Spiiiinn. Click.

"Y'all hear that?" one dopeboy frowned, trying to make out the noise.

"Hear what?" another asked, straining to listen.

"Shhh. Turn the TV down," the first one insisted. Reese lowered the volume, and they all listened closely.

Spiiiinn. Click. Spiiiinn. Click. Spiiiinn. Click.

"There it is again!" the first dopeboy shouted. They scrambled for their hidden guns. But before they could cock them, boom. The door crashed inward.

Chick ran in like a desperado, a revolver in each hand, blowing niggaz away. One dopeboy took a bullet to the chest. He flipped over the kitchen table, knocking over all the drug paraphernalia. A second dopeboy caught a bullet in his mouth. He fell back on the couch dead, still holding his gun. Cordare took four in the torso. He crashed into the stove, knocking over the Pyrex pot on his way to the floor.

In seconds, Chick had cleared the room, except for Reese, who was frantically trying to unjam his Tec-9.

Chick crept up behind him and pressed her revolver against his temple. Reese froze and his eyes widened with terror. His weapon clattered to the floor.

"You Reese?" Chick asked, her voice soft and deadly, a contrast to Cowboy's gruff tone.

Reese blinked, stunned. The voice didn't match the figure he knew as Cowboy. He nodded slowly. "Yeah, that's me."

"You know my son, Cowboy?" Chick's eyes narrowed.

Reese wanted to say, *mothafucka you are Cowboy*, but thought better of it. Instead, he nodded. "Yes, ma'am. He's the one who gave me this designer bag," he said, glancing at his colostomy bag.

Chick's eyes darted to the bag. "Come on, lil' man. We're goin' for a ride."

Reese swallowed the lump of fear in his throat, as he was led out at gunpoint.

***

"You know how to drive, kid?" Chick asked as they approached the car.

"Yeah," Reese answered.

"You're driving," she said, opening the passenger door and motioning for him to get in.

"Where are we going?"

"Your spot."

"For what?"

Chick didn't say a word. She slammed the passenger door shut; her eyes locked on him, and gestured with the barrel of her pistol for him to start the engine. Reese, swallowing his nerves, did as he was told. The car pulled away, and a heavy silence fell between them, stretching out like the road ahead.

The drive was suffocatingly quiet. Reese could feel the sweat beading on his forehead, his stomach churning. He kept glancing over at Chick, her face calm, almost bored, her finger resting lightly on the trigger. The silence was a noose tightening around his neck. He couldn't take it anymore. He had to break the tension, He had to know what she had planned.

Clearing his throat, Reese finally blurted out, "A-are you gonna, gonna kill me?"

Chick kept her Peacemaker aimed steadily at him, her face unreadable, her silence more unnerving than any threat. Minutes ticked by, each second stretching longer than the last, before she finally spoke.

"Why don't you tell me about your upbringing? Tell me what led you to being in these streets."

Reese exhaled, relieved to have something to say. "Where do I begin?"

He gave Chick the rundown of his life—the hard knocks, the losses, the choices he made that brought him to this point. Chick nodded occasionally, her face impassive, but her eyes sharp, taking in every word. By the time Reese pulled up to the projects, he had laid it all out.

"What do you want to be when you graduate high school?" she asked.

The question took Reese by surprise. A smile crept onto his face, softening his hardened expression. "I wanna be a mechanic. I love cars. I used to work on 'em with my pops before he passed."

"What's your ideal car?" Chick asked, genuine curiosity flickering in her eyes.

"A 1948 Chevy Fleetline," he replied quickly. "You know, a Bomber, one of those old cars that sit really low to the ground."

"Yeah, I know what you're talking about," she said, nodding. "I thought you were gonna say a Hellcat or a Bentley or some bullshit."

"Nah," Reese replied, shaking his head, his nose wrinkling at the thought. "Modern cars aren't my style."

Chick directed him to park and step out. As he did, the realization of his situation hit him again, his mood shifted back to wary. She led him to the trunk, and as she opened it, she saw him squeeze his eyes shut and mouth a silent prayer. Chick smirked, seeing the fear in his posture. She tucked her pistol and pulled out her last heavy sack of money, passing it to him. "Take this," she said. "Use it to pay for school, buy your dream ride, and get the hell outta the hood."

Reese's eyes widened. He looked down at the money, then back at her. "I thought you were gonna kill me," he whispered, voice barely above a breath.

Chick chuckled softly. "The thought never crossed my mind," she replied. "You get your family and make sure y'all get outta here. You're the oldest, so you're the man of the house. Make it happen."

Reese watched as she reloaded her Peacemaker revolvers, his eyes widening further when he realized they were both empty. She never intended to harm him. "I want chu to take this," she continued, pressing the loaded gun into his hand and holstering the other. "Protect what's yours. That's a lotta money you got there, and living in this place," she glanced at the towering buildings of the projects, "you're gonna need a piece to fend off the vultures."

Reese nodded, looking around nervously before tucking the revolver into his waistband. Then, without warning, he flung his arms around Chick, tears streaming down his cheeks. "Thank you," he whispered, his voice choked with emotion.

Imagining him as a thirteen-year-old Cowboy, Chick hugged him and rubbed his head. "Don't let me down."

He nodded with a fierce determination in his eyes. "I won't."

"One more thing," she said, removing the wide-brimmed hat and adjusting it on his head. "There you go, just perfect. It's almost like it was made for you."

Reese smiled happily. Chick watched as he dashed towards his building and disappeared through the entrance. The small smile that emerged on her face seconds ago melted away. It was replaced by a cold, focused expression. She slid her sunglasses back on and her face hardened.

It was time to get down to business.

Chapter 9

Remo and Lou stood in front of his whip, their eyes narrowing as the bright headlights of a Tahoe truck pierced through the darkness of the warehouse. The truck rattled from the loud music blaring out of its speakers. With a final rev of the engine, the SUV turned off, and the headlights dimmed. Parelli and Diamond jumped out, slamming their doors behind them, the sound echoing in the vast space. As they walked up to Remo and Lou, Lou's hand instinctively moved toward his waistband, but Remo stretched his arm across Lou's chest, stopping him.

"Relax, lil' nigga," Remo said, his gaze fixed on the approaching men. He then locked eyes with Parelli. "Yo, where the fuck is Rich?"

"Rich had some business to take care of, bruh. So, he sent me," Parelli replied coolly.

Remo's jaw tightened. He hated to hear this. He had been looking forward to taking down Rich Loc to fulfill his end of the deal with Golden. But now, that plan had to be put on hold for business.

"You got that work?" Remo asked, trying to keep his frustration in check.

"You got that money?" Parelli shot back.

"It's nearby," Remo said with a measured tone.

"So is the product," Parelli responded, crossing his arms over his chest.

"Look, fam, before we make any exchange, I'ma need to test y'all shit to make sure it's the same merch that nigga Rich lemme get a bump off," Remo insisted, narrowing his eyes.

It's always something, Parelli thought, biting his lip and shaking his head. He glanced at his watch. *I'm supposed to pick up my BM for physical therapy in thirty minutes.*

"Look, it's the same shit as always," Parelli told him, exasperation seeping into his voice. "Same connect. Same product. Take it from me."

"My nigga, the only thing I'ma take from you is the same work as ya boss lemme get a sample of," Remo retorted. "You can keep the rest of that bullshit."

Parelli rolled his eyes and let out a heavy sigh. He nudged Diamond, who took the signal and jogged to the Tahoe. Diamond returned with a small, tightly wrapped package, one of the birds they planned on selling to Remo.

Diamond handed the package to Parelli, who tossed it to Remo. Remo caught it with one hand and signaled Lou to check it out. Lou pulled out a small knife and made a small incision in the package. He dipped a finger in, brought it to his nose, and sniffed. Then he tasted a tiny amount, his face scrunching.

"It's legit," Lou confirmed, nodding to Remo.

"Yo, Lou," Remo said, not taking his eyes off Parelli. "Get that loot outta the car."

Lou nodded and walked back to the car. Moments later, he returned with an army bag.

Bloom.

The army bag ripped open and lifted a surprised Diamond off his feet. Lou came out of the bag with a nickel-plated pump-action shotgun. He racked it, and let it roar again, striking Diamond high in the chest. Diamond crashed to the pavement dead, blood pouring out of his wounds and pooling around him.

Parelli reached for his gun, but Remo was faster, drawing his heat and aiming it at him. "You know what, I think I'ma take all that product you got on the house," Remo said coldly. "I take it the rest of it is in yo' ride over there?"

Parelli hesitated, his eyes darting to the Tahoe. Remo cocked the hammer on his gun, and Parelli reluctantly nodded.

"Good," Remo smiled sinisterly. "Let's take a walk."

Remo kept his gun trained on Parelli as he escorted him to the truck. "Show me the merch," Remo ordered.

Parelli opened the back of the Tahoe, revealing a large duffle bag stuffed with neatly wrapped packages. Remo's eyes gleamed with satisfaction.

"Nice doing business with chu," Remo said, pushing Parelli aside and unzipping the bag to confirm the contents. He was about to pull the trigger and end Parelli when he reconsidered. If he forced Parelli to show him where the rest of the drugs were and where Rich Loc was held up, he could cut the head off the snake entirely.

"You're coming with me," Remo decided. "You're gonna show me where the rest of the stash is and where Rich is laying his head."

Parelli frowned. "I ain't tellin' you shit," he spat.

Remo pressed the barrel of his gun to Parelli's forehead. "Come again."

A few years ago, Parelli would have gladly died behind his beliefs, but now he had a girl and a son to think about. He didn't want to leave either of them alone in the world, so he was forced to submit.

Parelli's eyes flickered with fear and desperation. He thought about his family and the life he wanted to give them. Slowly, he nodded. "Alright, I'll show you."

Remo smirked, satisfied with the answer. "Good choice. Now get in the Tahoe."

Parelli climbed into the driver's seat of the Tahoe, and Remo slid in beside him, keeping his gun trained on him.

"Lou, follow us in your whip," Remo ordered.

Lou nodded, getting into the car and starting the engine. Remo's mind was focused on the bigger picture as they drove out of the warehouse. With Parelli as his guide, he was one step closer to finding Rich Loc and taking over his operation. It was a risky play, but Remo thrived on risk. And tonight, he was all in.

***

Unbeknownst to Remo and Lou, Hush and Boodee sat parked outside the warehouse, watching them leave. Hush, on FaceTime with Wood, whispered into the phone, "I just saw Remo and his boy leave."

Wood's voice crackled through the speaker; urgency evident in his tone. "Follow Remo. Don't lose 'em."

Hush nodded, ending the call. He turned to Boodee. "You heard 'em. Let's move."

They started the engine and followed Remo and Lou at a safe distance, careful not to be noticed.

***

Remo and Lou escorted Parelli inside the industrial laundromat. The place was humid, filled with the constant hum of machines and the hiss of rising steam. They walked past Japanese workers conversing in their language, all dressed in white, with hair coverings and aprons. Remo and Lou avoided eye contact, hiding their faces until they reached the supply room. Remo handed Parelli his keys, and Parelli unlocked the door, leading them inside.

The room was dimly lit and cluttered with cleaning supplies and equipment. Parelli walked over to a seemingly ordinary shelf and activated a hidden switch. The shelf slid aside, revealing a stash of neatly wrapped packages of cocaine. He grabbed a black garbage bag and began filling it with the kilos.

Lou kept his shotgun trained on Parelli, while Remo watched, wearing a satisfied smirk. "Make it quick," Remo barked. "We ain't got all day."

Parelli worked faster, the bag filling up with valuable packages. Parelli reached for the next package, but instead of grabbing the drugs, he reached for a gun stashed out of sight for emergencies. In one swift motion, he snapped around and shot Lou in the face. Lou collapsed to the floor, dead before he hit the surface.

Remo, reacting in a split second, blasted Parelli in the chest. Parelli fell back, gasping for breath, blood pooling around him. Remo kept his gun pinned on him as he walked up, seeing the life drain from Parelli's eyes.

"Shit. Shit. Shit," Remo repeated, realizing his chances of getting his hands on Rich Loc were slipping away. An idea struck him. He pulled out Parelli's cellphone and used face recognition to unlock it. Quickly navigating to Rich Loc's contact, he sent a text.

"Yo, it's Parelli. I ran into Golden. We need to meet ASAP."

Moments later, a reply came through. "Where?"

Remo shot Rich Loc the location he had in mind, telling him to meet him there in an hour.

Rich Loc replied, "Bet."

Remo sent a text message to Golden to let him know what was good. Then he finished filling the garbage bag with the work and walked out of the supply room, wiping blood from his face. He glanced back at Lou's lifeless body and a pang of regret hit him. But he couldn't afford to mourn now. He had to keep moving.

As he exited the laundromat, the humid night air hit him like a wrecking ball. He took a deep breath and tried to steady his nerves. The adrenaline was still pumping through him. He couldn't afford any mistakes now. He returned to his ride with the garbage bag slung over his shoulder. He had just the place in mind to stash the product until he got Rich Loc out of the way.

***

Sitting behind the tinted windows of Parelli's Tahoe, Remo checked Parelli's cellphone for the hundredth time in forty-five minutes. He was supposed to link up with Rich Loc at the specified location, but Rich was nowhere to be seen. Suspicion gnawed at him. Something was off. Just as he decided to pull off, he sent one more text to Rich Loc.

"Yo, son, where you at? I've been out here mad long."

Rich Loc replied, "My bad, crip. I ran into a lil' sitch, but I'm pulling up now."

Remo glanced in his sideview mirror and saw a tinted royal blue '64 Chevy Impala coasting up. A wicked smile spread across his face as he reclined his seat and rolled down the driver's side window. The moment the Chevy stopped alongside Parelli's whip; Remo emptied the entire clip through the front passenger window. He quickly hopped out, reloaded, and jogged to the driver's door. He raised his gun to blast the driver's side of the windshield and got the surprise of a lifetime.

Poc. Poc. Poc. Poc.

Remo, looking bewildered, ducked low and retreated from the gunfire. Rich Loc, who had the driver's seat reclined all the way back, threw open the door and followed him, firing relentlessly.

Poc. Poc. Poc. Poc.

"You thought you could set me up, cuz? That'll be the day The Loc lets a ho-ass nigga like you be his downfall."

Remo didn't know it but Rich Loc's industrial laundry mat had secret surveillance cameras, so he could see what was going on at all times. He saw him kill Parelli and send the text for their meeting. He had been on to Remo the entire time.

Remo ducked behind Parelli's Tahoe, his heart thudding. He fired back blindly, bullets and sparks ricocheting off the Impala's hood. "You got it all wrong, Loc. I wasn't trying to—"

Another rush of gunfire cut him off, forcing him to huddle tighter against the vehicle. He had walked right into a trap.

Rich Loc's voice echoed through the chaos. "You ain't leaving here alive, Remo."

Remo knew he had to act fast. He reloaded and took a deep breath, steeling himself for the next move. In a desperate dash, he sprinted to the back of the Tahoe, using it as cover as he fired at Rich Loc. The gunfight was brutal, and it wouldn't be long before he ran out of ammo. Rich Loc, on the other hand, appeared to have some shit with an unlimited number of bullets.

Remo needed a way out, but the relentless gunfire from Rich Loc kept him pinned down. His eyes darted around, searching for a place he could run and put some distance between them. That way he could flee and formulate another plan to get at his opp.

Remo grinned when his eyes landed on the entrance of an alley. As he prepared to make a run for it, J-Bo emerged from the shadows, busting his gun. Remo fell on his back in his attempt to avoid the bullets meant for his knot. He looked over his shoulder. Rich Loc was running in his direction to put something hot in his chest. He had a look on his face that Remo read as *I got this nigga now.*

Remo looked above his head and J-Bo was easing up on him too. Remo's heart thumped in his chest. The walls were closing in on him fast. He was far too young to die, so he was going to fight for his. He sent fire in Rich Loc and J-Bo's direction, backing them down. He rolled aside, scrambled back up, and took off running. J-Bo and Rich Loc slowly emerged from hiding, joined forces, and went after Remo.

Chapter 10

Remo would duck behind a parked car now and again, blasting at J-Bo and Rich Loc, keeping them off his ass. At his last stop, he pointed his stick at them and pulled the trigger once.

Click.

Remo frowned as he looked at his gun. He pointed it back at the opposition and pulled the trigger twice.

Click Click.

He was out of bullets. Fuck! Remo threw his stick aside, hopped up, and ran down the street. J-Bo and Rich Loc gave chase, busting at him. He ducked low, zig-zagging as he ran, bullets whizzing around him.

Remo looked like he was going to shit his pants when two masked gunmen ran out in front of him. They pointed their guns at him and one of them yelled, "Get down."

Remo dived to the sidewalk and the masked gunmen started spitting fire.

Blocka. Blocka. Blocka. Blocka.

J-Bo got a chest and a stomach full of bullets while Rich Loc ran behind a car for cover. J-Bo collapsed, staring at him in horror as his life's blood expanded around him. Seeing he didn't stand a chance against two shooters, Rich Loc stayed low and retreated to his whip.

The masked gunmen pulled Remo up by his arms and escorted him toward their truck. He looked from left to right, wondering who they were.

"I owe y'all niggaz one, on God. Y'all saved my ass," Remo said. "Them dudes had me dead to rights."

"Shut the fuck up, Remo," one of the masked gunmen said.

Remo frowned as he recognized the voice. "Boodee?" The masked gunman didn't say shit, so he knew he was right. He looked at the masked gunman opposite of him. If given the chance, he'd bet his right arm he was Hush. "Hush?"

"You're smarter than you look, dick," Hush replied.

Remo swallowed the lump of fear in his throat. He had a feeling he was about to be in a bad way. Instantly, his mind raced with ways he could get out of his situation.

"There isn't shit you can say to get outta us taking you to holla at Wood, Remo," Hush stated, as if he had just read Remo's mind. "If I know yo' punk-ass, the gears are turning in that head of yours."

"What, uh, what does Wood want with me?" Remo asked, looking at Hush and then Boodee, hoping one of them would answer his inquiring mind.

"You'll find out once we get there," Boodee whacked him across the back of his skull with his gun. Remo fell into Hush's arms unconscious.

"Yo' grab the duct tape outta the glove box so we can gift wrap that fool," Hush told Boodee. "And this time we dumpin' 'em in the hatch."

Boodee followed instructions. He returned, pulling a length of duct tape from its roll.

***

Remo frowned as he stirred awake to a pounding headache. He blinked the haze from his eyes and took in his surroundings. He was in an old Wonder Bread factory that had been abandoned for years. Dust and cobwebs clung to the rusted machinery, and the occasional rat scurried along the grimy walls. The sound of locks being undone caught his attention, drawing his eyes to the door before him. It swung open, casting a blinding light into the room. He squinted, straining to see the figures that entered.

Two dark silhouettes stepped inside, flanking the door with assault rifles at the ready. A third figure sauntered in, whistling a tuneless melody. Remo recognized the figure as the light adjusted and felt a chill run down his spine. It was Wood, holding LaCresha, his beloved machete, with a deadly casualness.

"Morning, Remo," Wood said with a sinister grin, dragging LaCresha along Remo's body. "Sleep well?"

"Wood," Remo spat, trying to sound defiant despite the fear gnawing at him.

Wood chuckled, circling Remo slowly. "Let's cut to the chase. Did you pop Trell back at the cookhouse?"

Remo shook his head vehemently. "I don't know what you're talking about."

Wood's eyes narrowed. "Come on, Remo. Don't be a bitch-ass nigga all yo' life. We both know you don't have the stones to take out Trell, without pissing yourself at the thought of what his old man would do to you."

Anger flared in Remo's eyes. "You don't know shit about me," he snapped. "Yeah, I took Trell out. Put a bullet right between his eyes. And you know what? I'd do it again."

Wood's smile widened, and his eyes showed a cruel, predatory gleam. "There we go. Now we're getting somewhere." He glanced at Hush and Boodee, who stood by the door, silently watching. "Y'all hear that? Remo thinks he's a big man."

Remo forced a laugh, his bravado returning. "You think my boys aren't gonna come for me? They're probably right outside, ready to blow this place to hell and back."

Wood raised an eyebrow, clearly amused. "How long you think it'll take for yo' squad to get here?"

"Any minute now," Remo replied, trying to keep the tremor out of his voice.

Wood nodded thoughtfully. "Alright then. I'll give you three minutes." He set his watch and leaned against a dusty piece of machinery, chatting with Hush and Boodee, as if they were old friends.

Seconds ticked by, each one an eternity. Sweat beaded on Remo's forehead as he strained to hear any sign of his rescuers. The silence was deafening, and with each passing moment, his confidence waned.

Finally, Wood's watch beeped. He silenced it and pushed himself off the machinery, strolling over to Remo with LaCresha resting on his shoulder. "Time's up, sweetheart."

Remo's facade crumbled. "Wait, please. We can work something out. I can give you information, money, anything you want."

Wood's face darkened, and his smile turned cold. "Too late for that, Remo."

With a swift, brutal motion, Wood brought LaCresha down, burying the machete halfway into Remo's head. Blood poured down his face as he slumped forward. Wood kicked the chair, toppling Remo to the ground. Straddling his twitching body, Wood hacked away with relentless ferocity, his face and clothes splattered with blood.

When it was done, Wood stood, wiping his face and smearing the blood further. He turned to Hush and Boodee. "Clean this nigga up."

Wood pulled a bandana out of his right back pocket. He wiped the blood off his face and then LaCresha. Sheathing the machete on his hip, he picked up the cellphone he'd propped against one of the old machines to film his interaction with Remo. Stepping outside, he sent the footage of Remo's confession and demise to Chaka. He posted outside the factory and waited for an associate of his to arrive. By the time his associate pulled up, he got a FaceTime call from Chaka. He exchanged greetings with his glassy-eyed elder and he thanked Wood for avenging his son's death.

"You did right by Trell, Woody," Chaka said. "I can finally rest, knowing my boy's been avenged. You be sure to come and visit me soon, a'ight?"

"I gotchu," Wood replied.

"I love you, son," Chaka said.

"I love you too, unc," Wood disconnected the call as Golden approached. He took note of the cuts and bruises on his face but didn't bother acknowledging it.

Golden handed him a backpack. "Five birds, just like I promised," he said. "We straight now?"

Wood unzipped the backpack and revealed five neatly packaged birds of raw cocaine.

Wood, expression serious, nodded. "Yeah, we're good now. My word."

Golden made a deal with Wood. He would give him Remo and five bricks, if he agreed to squash their beef. Golden got the fifteen bricks Remo stole from Rich Loc. He kept ten for himself and kicked the other five up to Wood, so he didn't take a loss. He gained with this transaction.

Golden dapped up Wood, hopped back in his whip, and drove away. He adjusted his rearview mirror and saw Hush and Boodee carrying suitcases. He wasn't really a gambling man, but he'd bet his left nut those suitcases had Remo's remains in them.

***

Now that the situation with Wood was behind him, Golden decided to spend the next two hours searching for Cowboy. He hit every spot he thought he'd likely be, but he wasn't at any of them. Just when he was about to slide to the armory to holler at the twins and his mother, his cellphone chimed with a text message. He was surprised when he saw who it was.

Rich Loc: "I know who you are. I know what you meant to Aries. Let's get this shit out the way. Just you and me. Bring yo' stick."

Golden's eyes narrowed as tension built in his chest. He shot back, "A'ight, bet." His thoughts swam the entire drive to his destination, trying to figure out a strategy to crush Rich Loc. He couldn't come up with anything solid. So, he decided to bring it to him head-on.

Golden had been in more shootouts than he cared to count, and each one had left its mark. But no matter how many times he went up against another gun, that familiar feeling of dread never left him. He could feel it now, nervousness gnawing at his gut, his heart thudding in his chest, hands slick with sweat. Sitting outside Rich Loc's mansion, his car idling, Golden was aware that he was stepping into a fight where the odds were stacked high against him. But he didn't care. He was done playing games. Rich Loc needed to be put in the ground, and Golden was ready to do it.

He checked his gear one last time. Hood pulled low, black sunglasses masking his eyes, a bulletproof vest strapped tight to his chest, and a Glock resting heavily in his lap, loaded with a 30-round clip and equipped with a switch. Everything was in place.

Golden threw the car into drive and floored the gas. His knuckles whitened as he gripped the steering wheel, eyes flicking between the climbing needle on the speedometer and the looming twin doors of Rich Loc's estate.

Ba-Doom.

He crashed through the front entrance, the force of impact sending splintered wood, plaster, and debris flying in all directions. The air filled with dust, but Golden was already moving. He jumped out of the car, gun at the ready, and pushed forward, his senses on high alert.

The mansion was a palace of opulence, the kind of place that dripped with wealth. Golden barely glanced at the enormous water fountain adorned with a nine-foot statue of Rich Loc himself, or the Italian paintings and imported furniture that cost more than most people's homes. He was on a mission, and the only thing on his mind was putting an end to Rich Loc, once and for all.

He sprinted up the grand staircase, checking every room he passed. But the house was empty, eerily so.

Where the fuck is this mothafucka? he thought, his frustration mounting.

Then he heard it. Voices echo from deep within the mansion, growing louder with every step. He followed them down a hallway that stretched endlessly, the walls lined with ornate mirrors that reflected his tense expression.

The voices led him to a secluded foyer. The space was decked out with framed movie posters, burgundy leather furniture that looked worn from years of use, and a popcorn maker that was busy filling the room with the smell of fresh buttered kernels. Next to it were twin doors. Behind them, Golden knew, was Rich Loc.

He took a deep breath, adjusted his grip on the Glock, and pushed the doors open. The sound hit him first, Dolby surround, crystal clear, so loud it felt like he'd stepped into a theater. On the massive screen, Aries was creeping up behind Rich Loc, steak knife in hand. But when it came time to strike, she hesitated. The steak knife fell to the floor, and the next scene showed Rich Loc and Aries tangled together on a couch, bodies moving in rhythm.

Golden's blood ran cold. Scene after scene played out, showing the betrayal in excruciating detail. Then came the kicker. Diamond, disguised as a cable guy, installing hidden cameras throughout the house. He'd even joked with Aries about taking out the trash on his way out. Rich Loc knew everything. The thought slammed into Golden like a freight train. He'd known every step of the way and had played them all for fools.

Chapter 11

Golden's gaze snapped to the center of the theater. There, in the middle row, sat Rich Loc. He looked relaxed, almost casual, as he stuffed his face with popcorn and sipped on a cherry slushy, eyes fixed on the screen, as if he were just another moviegoer.

"You gotta hand it to our girl, Golden," Rich Loc finally spoke, his voice calm, eyes still glued to the screen. "Shorty deserves an Oscar or a Grammy or something, cuz. Word is bond."

Golden didn't respond, his body tense, eyes narrowing behind his sunglasses.

The screen flickered to another scene—Aries' driver's license in full view, her real name highlighted. Golden's heart dropped. This wasn't a game anymore. This was real, and Rich Loc had been pulling the strings all along.

"Who you think the bitch truly loved outta the two of us?" Rich Loc asked, still not looking back. His voice was almost conversational, like he was discussing the weather. "You don't know, huh? Go ahead, take a stab at it, my nigga. I couldn't tell you for sho', but I think she really loved you. Maybe I shoulda asked her that before I jumped the gun and killed her."

Golden's eyes bubbled in shock upon hearing Rich Loc's revelation.

***

Rich Loc entered Aries's hospital room, pausing at the door as her nurse finished checking her vitals. The nurse, noticing him, smiled warmly. "Looks like you've got a visitor, girl. Is that your man? He's handsome," she whispered the last part in Aries's ear. "I'll leave you two alone, be back later to check on you," she said, giving Aries's arm an affectionate rub before walking toward the door. She introduced herself as Aries's nurse, Sha'rye, and shook Rich Loc's hand. He introduced himself as Richard, maintaining a polite smile as he watched her leave.

"Hey, baby," Rich Loc greeted softly, kissing Aries's cheek. Sha'rye glanced back with an "aww" look on her face, appreciating the tender moment. But as soon as she left, Rich Loc's demeanor shifted. He gently caressed Aries's forehead; his touch cold despite the softness.

"You're a grimy-ass bitch, you know that, Gabby, or should I say Aries?" he snarled, his voice dripping with venom.

Pow.

His fist crashed into her stomach. Aries, despite her coma, faintly frowned, her body reacting to the violent intrusion.

Pow. Pow. Pow.

He continued to pound her abdomen relentlessly. "I saw and heard everything through the surveillance cameras and wiretaps that bogus-ass cable man hooked up. By the way, bitch, that was my nigga, Diamond." He landed another brutal punch. His anger was fierce, but he kept himself from striking her face, not wanting to leave visible bruises.

"You fucking whore. I gave you my heart, and what did you do? You stomped all over it." His voice cracked, but he quickly wiped away the tears that threatened to spill. He checked the hallway, ensuring the staff were busy, before ducking back into the room. His rage reignited as he yanked the pillow from under her head and mashed it against her face.

"You fucking bitch, I fucking hate chu. How could you do this to me? I loved you. I fucking loved you. I-I still do," he choked out, tears streaming down his face as he removed the pillow, revealing her still features. His breath hitched as he checked her pulse, his fingers trembling against her neck. Nothing. A dark satisfaction mixed with sorrow washed over him as he realized she was gone.

Rich Loc wiped his tear-stained face with his sleeve, sniffling as he tried to compose himself. He tucked the pillow behind her head and cleared his throat to prepare for his next act. "Oh, my God, baby," he screamed, running to the door and shouting for the staff, his voice laced with frantic urgency.

The staff came rushing down the hallway, their footsteps echoing in the corridor, unaware of the horror that had just unfolded behind the door.

***

Rich Loc's feet felt like they were weighed down by his guilt as he trudged through the dimly lit parking garage. His head hung low, each step echoing the turmoil inside him. He climbed into his car and slammed the door shut. He abruptly pounded his fist against the steering wheel, each blow fueled by a self-loathing that clawed at his insides. The rage bubbled over, but even through the storm of his emotions, he knew deep down that if he could take back what he'd done to Aries, he wouldn't.

"You see, girl? You see what you made me do?" Rich Loc's voice trembled as he stared up at the ceiling, tears streaming down his face. The sound of his voice broke him, a mix of anger and sorrow. "All this shit behind that punk-ass nigga Golden. Some broke-ass muthafucka that gotta stick ballaz up just to get his? We were beautiful together. I laid the world at yo' feet, and you pissed on it."

He bowed his head, his shoulders shaking violently as he wept. His tears soaked into his shirt, but the pain was too deep to be washed away by something as simple as crying. At that moment, the weight of his actions pressed down on him like a mountain, but the darkness within him whispered that he'd do it all over again. Aries was gone, and so was a part of him he could never get back.

***

Tears welled up in Rich Loc's eyes, spilling onto his cheeks as he spoke. He was a man unraveling, but Golden wasn't moved. He stood at the entrance, the Glock steady in his hand, staring down at the man who had caused so much pain. Tears slowly burst from his eyes and slid down his cheeks.

Suddenly, Rich Loc hurled his bucket of popcorn at him. As Golden went to dodge it, he upped two golden .45 automatics, popping off like a madman, shell casings flying over his shoulders.

Golden dove behind a row of theater seats, narrowly missing the bullets meant to take his head off his shoulders. His adrenaline ran rampant through his veins as his heart raced crazily. He strained his eyes trying to find a line of sight on Rich Loc's ankles beneath the seats, but there was no clear shot.

"Fuck," he muttered under his breath, trying to figure out his next move.

Rich Loc, eerily calm, stalked up the aisle. On the massive screen behind him, Aries professed her love for him after they'd made love, but he paid it no mind. His focus was solely on ending Golden's life.

"This is personal, cuz," Rich Loc snarled, tears streaming down his face as he scanned the dark theater for any sign of Golden. "You took my money, my bitch, and my happiness. So, it's only right that The Loc takes yo' life."

Poc. Poc. Poc. Poc. Poc.

Rich Loc squeezed the triggers of his twin .45s, sending bullets tearing through the theater seats, ripping them apart, and sending debris flying. Golden popped up to Rich Loc's far right, sprinting toward the theater's entrance, while firing blindly behind him. Rich Loc responded with another barrage, shattering the glass of the popcorn maker and striking Golden's shoulder. Golden howled in pain as he stumbled into the doorway, desperately pushing himself forward.

On the screen, another scene played of Aries whispering "I love you" to Rich Loc, fueling his fury. Enraged, Rich Loc turned and emptied his magazines into the enormous screen, plunging the theater into complete darkness. Reloading his pistols with a swift practiced motion, he stormed out of the theater, telling the story of how he and Aries first met, realizing too late that he'd been nothing more than a mark to her from the start.

Rich Loc activated a mechanism on his identical pistols and secured their slides in place. As he entered the foyer, he tucked one .45 under his arm and pulled out his cellphone, bringing up the full layout of his mansion on the screen. He noticed a thermal reading in the kitchen and zoomed in. Golden was crouched behind the counter, his gun lowered, preparing for the showdown.

A wicked smile spread across Rich Loc's face. With murder on his brain, he pocketed his cellphone and took off down the hallway in the opposite direction.

***

Golden, still hidden behind the kitchen counter, frowned as he realized the eerie silence that had fallen. He was keenly aware that he was at Rich Loc's mercy, deep in enemy territory. The thought of being a cornered rat crossed his mind, but he dismissed it, pushing himself to stay sharp.

Inspecting his shoulder wound, he cursed under his breath at the sight of the blood that collected on the floor. The bullet had done more than graze him, it had lodged deep, and he was losing blood fast. He needed to move, but as he prepared to make his next move, Rich Loc emerged from the pantry behind him, through a hidden trapdoor connected to the mansion's study.

Before Golden could react, Rich Loc leveled his pistols and fired. Golden crumpled to the floor and his gun skidded out of reach. The fire of the bullets seared through his back and left him gasping in agony. Tears welled in his eyes as he struggled to turn over, looking up at Rich Loc, who approached with a wicked smile.

"Gotcha," Rich Loc sneered, blowing a kiss at Golden. He raised his sticks, ready to deliver the final shots. "Say goodnight, bitch boy."

Golden, voice trembling with pain and defeat, stammered, "Go, go ahead, nigga. K-kill me. I wanna be with my lady anyway. I'm, I'm tired of fuckin' around with yo' ass."

Rich Loc's fury reignited at Golden's words. "No. Aries is mine. You had her in this life, but she'll be all mine in death."

Rich Loc pressed both his weapons under his chin and pulled their triggers. Blood and gore erupted through the ceiling of his skull. His world went black as he collapsed to the kitchen floor, his .45s lying on either side of him, smoking.

Gritting his teeth, Golden pushed up from the floor, staring at what was left of Rich Loc.

I guess it's true what they say, Golden thought bitterly, wiping specks of blood from his face. *Love will make you do some crazy thangs.*

Grabbing his gun, he made his way up the grand staircase to the bathroom, where he removed his hoodie and bulletproof vest. Through his reflection in the mirror, he examined the ugly, awful bruising on his back, evidence of the close-range gunfire.

Golden cleaned and bandaged his shoulder wound as best as he could. He rifled through the medicine cabinet, finding some prescription Perc 30s, which he swallowed dry, wincing as they went down. The painkillers would take the edge off.

Golden walked back down the stairs and into the kitchen. He took one last look at Rich Loc's mangled skull. He wondered if the dopeboy loved Aries more than him. And if she, in turn, loved Rich Loc more than she loved him. Realizing he'd never get the answer to his question, he took an exasperated breath and walked out of the mansion. Oblivious to the huge portrait over the fireplace of Rich Loc and Aries smiling as they stared into each other's eyes, seeming madly in love.

***

Golden climbed back behind the wheel of his car and programmed its navigation system for the armory. Little did he know, upon his arrival, that his entire world would be rocked down to its core.

***

The football game went to halftime so Heavy returned to his cell to see if he'd gotten any messages. Keeping an eye out, he discreetly took his contraband cellphone from its hiding place and powered it on. It vibrated immediately with a call from an unfamiliar number. He squinted at the screen, frowning. *Who the hell could this be?* After a moment of hesitation, he pressed the answer button. "Yeah?"

"What up, old man?" Cowboy's voice came through, light and casual, catching Heavy off guard.

Heavy's jaw tightened. He didn't trust this. He leaned back in his chair, clearing his throat, trying to mask his wariness. "Aye, what it do, son?"

"Nothin' much. Just seein' what chu on," Cowboy replied smoothly.

Heavy forced a chuckle, playing along. "Just doin' a lil' readin', that's all," he said, removing his glasses and setting his book aside, eyes narrowing slightly as he tried to read the intent behind Cowboy's words.

Cowboy eased into small talk, chatting about sports, the weather, women, family, stuff that usually wouldn't be worth a damn, but something in Cowboy's voice was off. It was too casual, too controlled. Heavy felt the tension coil tight in his gut.

Then Cowboy shifted gears, his tone changing ever so slightly. "Speakin' of family, I can't seem to get ahold of ma, the twins, or G," he said. "I was hopin' to holla at them so we could hash thangs out. You know where they're holed up?"

"I'm glad you wanna make amends with the family, Junior. We're all we've got."

"No doubt."

"Gemme a second," Heavy said calmly. He texted Cowboy the address where Shirvetta and the twins were. "Sent."

"Thanks, pop."

"You're welcome. I love you, son."

"I love you, too, Daddy," Cowboy replied.

Heavy's heart skipped a beat. Cowboy sounded eerily like his mother, Chick.

"Chick?" Heavy muttered in confusion, but Cowboy had already hung up.

Pushing the interaction to the back of his brain, Heavy stashed his contraband cellphone, and hit the yard.

Chapter 12

Shirvetta washed her hands as she stared at her reflection in the bathroom mirror. Her mind was racing with the weight of everything she'd done. She had just gotten a call from Dr. Abagnale, who mentioned that he and his wife, his surgical assistant, would be arriving shortly. The thought of going under the knife had her a little shaken, but it wasn't the surgery itself that scared her. It was the anesthesia. The idea of being put to sleep and possibly not waking up again clawed at her nerves.

She wasn't about to lie to herself; she wasn't anybody's angel. If she was honest, she was closer to being a demon. She had done shit, dark shit, shit she knew God wouldn't forgive. She could try and convince herself that everything was out of necessity, but that would be a lie. No, most of the things she'd done were just pure evil.

She had killed Cowboy's mother, just to have Heavy to herself. Manipulating him into helping her get rid of the body had been too easy. The cold part about it? She didn't even love Heavy like she claimed to. It was never about love for her. It was about not letting Chick have him. Chick, her so-called bestie, always had the upper hand, the finest niggaz, the better looks, and the attention. Shirvetta had to settle for whoever was left. Chick had the curves, the longer, softer hair, and even the better personality. Shirvetta hated that shit. She hated that she was always in second place.

But she finally got her win when she snatched Heavy right out from under Chick. Sure, it was trifling, killing her best friend over a man, but Shirvetta didn't give a fuck. Chick had always been in the spotlight, and for once, Shirvetta wanted to take something from her.

The memories of Chick still got to her sometimes. They were tight once, best friends since they were kids. Losing that bond over a nigga felt stupid now, but it was what it was. Shirvetta had to face the truth, she killed her sister over a man who wasn't even hers. And to make it worse, she didn't want Heavy after all was said and done. She only stuck with him because of their kids. Her hands were tied, or so she thought.

That changed when she met another man on the East Coast. Homie had her deep in her feelings. She was ready to risk it all behind him. He wasn't hers, but neither was Heavy when she went after him. So, she wasn't about to let that stop her.

Heavy had a hard time finding legit work when they first moved to New York, so he went back to sticking up street niggaz, just to make sure the rent got paid and food was on the table for his wife and four kids. The cheese he made was enough to get by, but it was nothing compared to the chips Shirvetta's side nigga was stacking. Her new boo was jacking kingpins and flipping work, and it didn't take long for Shirvetta to hatch a plan. If she could connect her main nigga with her side nigga, they'd be living like royalty. And that's exactly what she did, except she introduced her new boo as her cousin on her father's side to Heavy.

But once she was ready to leave Heavy, shit got complicated. She couldn't bring herself to tell her kids she was breaking up their home, so she schemed another way out. The next time her side nigga set up a lick, she would convince him to take out Heavy and keep the cash for themselves.

Everything seemed to go according to plan until the night Heavy was rolled into the hospital, still clinging to life. He had survived the bullet old boy put in his head. And when he came out of his coma, he wasn't just recovering, he was plotting his revenge.

***

Lump's heart was pounding in his chest when he hung up with Heavy. He had never moved so fast in his life. He leaped out of bed, startling Shirvetta, his side-bitch, who was lounging beside him, smoking a cigarette.

"Where you goin' inna hurry, Lump? I thought you were warmin' up for round two," Shirvetta asked, her voice tinged with irritation as she watched him scramble to get dressed.

"Yo' fuckin' husband done snatched up my wife, and he holdin' her for the loot we stole from 'em," Lump replied tersely as he pulled on his jeans and slipped his gun in his waistband. He grabbed his leather jacket, his mind racing with thoughts of Autumn and the danger she was in.

Shirvetta rolled her eyes, clearly unimpressed.

"Fuck you rollin' yo' eyes for?" Lump snapped, adjusting his navy-blue Yankees cap on his head.

"Why you playin' Captain Save-A-Ho now? You swore up and down you were leavin' that bitch for me anyway," Shirvetta argued, her voice dripping with contempt. "If dude wasted her, then that'll leave just you and me to be together, without alla the divorce court and alimony drama."

Lump stopped what he was doing and fixed her with a hard stare. "Understand this," he began, his voice low and dangerous, "I've been wit' my shorty since third grade. We got a different kinda love and understanding. I'm not finna just leave her to be handled whatever kinda way by this nigga."

Shirvetta waved him off dismissively, clearly not interested in his loyalty to his wife. She continued to smoke her cigarette, a bored expression on her face as Lump moved to the closet. He pulled down a briefcase and popped open the safe hidden inside. The sight of the money they had stolen, now stained with blood, filled him with a sense of dread. He quickly began loading the briefcase, his thoughts consumed with how he was going to get Autumn back alive.

As Lump zipped up the briefcase and grabbed his keys, casting one last glance at Shirvetta, she was still lying in bed, her cigarette smoldering in the ashtray beside her, a look of indifference on her face. He shook his head, knowing that there was no point in trying to explain the bond he had with Autumn to someone who would never understand.

Without another word, he left the room, his mind focused on the only thing that mattered—getting his wife back and making Heavy pay.

***

The front door rattled violently as someone pounded against it. "It's the police, open up."

"Oh, shit," Shirvetta cursed, bolting upright in bed. Heavy scrambled beside her, pulling on his jeans in a rush. Both of them knew what this meant. It wasn't just a visit.

Heavy darted to the closet, frantically grabbing kilos of cocaine wrapped in duct tape. His eyes scanned the room, his face pale with urgency. "I'm forgetting something," he muttered under his breath, scanning the mess of their bedroom.

"The guns. And the jewelry," Shirvetta hissed, her voice shaking but steady enough to keep her focused.

"We're on it, ma," Cowboy said, as he and Golden rushed past the bedroom door, Cowboy gripping a shotgun, and Golden with a backpack stuffed full of guns and ammo.

"Mommy, daddy, what's going on?" Biggie appeared in the doorway, clutching Baby Girl's hand. She was wiping sleep from her eyes, still gripping her stuffed animal tight against her chest.

"The Johnnies, son," Heavy growled as he handed Biggie two of the tightly wrapped kilos. "Remember the drill we practiced?"

Biggie nodded, his small arms taking the weight of the drugs without hesitation. Baby Girl let go of her stuffed animal and grabbed a couple more kilos, struggling but determined. They sprinted down the hallway toward their room to stash it, moving with an alarming level of discipline for kids their age.

Shirvetta tossed on her diamond necklaces and bracelets, covering them with her robe and tying it tight around her waist. She slipped on her fluffy rabbit slippers, her mind racing as she yelled toward the front door, "Just a second, I'm coming."

She glanced at Heavy. "You got everything?"

"I hope so," he muttered, pulling his tank top over his head, the tension clear in his voice.

Boom.

The front door exploded inward, slamming against the wall as police stormed inside, guns raised, shouting commands.

"Get on your knees. Hands up," the officers barked, their eyes cold and professional as they pointed their weapons at Heavy and Shirvetta.

"Is anyone else in the house?" the commanding officer asked, eyes narrowing as he looked them over.

"Just our kids, man. What the fuck is this about?" Heavy snapped as an officer yanked his arms behind his back and slapped on the handcuffs.

"Murder," the officer said flatly, tossing a warrant onto the floor beside Heavy. His tone was indifferent, as if he were talking about the weather.

A minute later, three cops stormed down the hallway, roughly dragging Cowboy and Golden into the living room.

Both boys struggled, faces flushed with anger. Behind them, another officer emerged, holding Baby Girl in his arms, her face wet with tears, while Biggie walked beside him, gripping his hand.

Shirvetta's heart sank at the sight of her kids in police custody. The chaos of their life had finally spilled over onto them.

***

Shirvetta turned off the faucet as cool water dripped from her hands. She looked back into the mirror and nearly jumped through the ceiling. The Grim Reaper stood behind her with a scythe, its deadly blade gleaming under the bathroom's harsh light. Her eyes widened in horror as he slowly pulled back his hood, revealing a face she hadn't seen in years but had haunted her dreams ever since, Chick.

Chick's smile was wicked, stretching her lips into a twisted, devilish expression. Her eyes burned with rage and satisfaction, as if she'd come back from the dead just to savor Shirvetta's fear. Shirvetta's heart plummeted into her stomach. Her mind raced as dread squeezed her insides, her past sins unraveling before her like a spool of yarn.

She spun around, trembling, but the bathroom was empty. Chick had vanished. The shower curtain billowed slightly, and Shirvetta lunged forward, yanking it back. There wasn't anyone there. She turned to the door. There wasn't anyone there either. She was alone.

Her chest heaved as panic gripped her like a pair of strong, masculine, calloused hands. She stumbled back, pressing herself against the bathroom wall, placing her hand over her heart, and desperately trying to slow her racing pulse. Chick couldn't be here. Chick was dead. Shirvetta had buried her deep beneath the lies and betrayal she had woven to cover up the murder. But the vision felt so real. Her hand quivered as she wiped her face and forced herself to breathe. She needed to calm the storm swirling in her mind.

"Bitch, you're losing it," she whispered to herself. But deep down, she couldn't shake the feeling that Chick wasn't done with her yet.

***

Biggie and Baby Girl were deep in it, arguing about whether they should snatch up Golden and torture him until he gave up Cowboy's whereabouts. Biggie was fired up, ready to go all in, while Baby Girl was against the plan. They'd gone back and forth for a while when the doorbell rang.

"That's probably the doc," Biggie said, raising his hand to silence Baby Girl. "I'll get the door. We'll settle this later."

***

Biggie opened the front door to find Dr. Abagnale and his wife, Shelby. Biggie dapped up the doctor and gave him a nod of respect. His exchange with Shelby was stiff. Mrs. Abagnale was clearly out of her element. Biggie noticed the awkwardness in her return dap and grinned, shaking his head. *White folks still ain't got it down.*

"Where's the patient?" Dr. Abagnale asked, looking around the room. He was ready to get down to business.

Biggie nodded toward the basement door. "This way."

They followed him down the hallway, where Biggie entered the security code to unlock the basement door. The heavy click echoed through the house, and they descended into the cool, dim basement. The air down there always felt a little heavier, a little more serious, like something bad could pop off at any second.

At the bottom of the stairs, Baby Girl was sitting next to Shirvetta, holding her hand. Shirvetta looked fragile but determined, a mix of nerves and resolve on her face, as she sat on the couch. Baby Girl wasn't saying much, but the tension in the room was thick enough to cut with a knife.

Dr. Abagnale and Shelby greeted Baby Girl and Shirvetta, exchanging a few words of comfort before the doctor got to work. He listened to Shirvetta's heart, checked her vitals, and gave her a reassuring smile.

"How are you feeling today, Ms. Shirvetta?" he asked, his tone soft, almost fatherly.

Shirvetta's voice came out steady, but one could hear the nerves underneath. "I'm a lil' scared, not gonna lie."

Dr. Abagnale nodded, packing away his stethoscope. "You've got nothing to worry about. We've done this a hundred times. You're in good hands."

He glanced toward the back room, the makeshift surgical space Biggie had set up. "That the room?"

Shirvetta nodded, and without another word, Dr. Abagnale reached into his sleek black bag, pulling out a hospital gown and hair covering for her. While she changed, Biggie led the doctor and Shelby to the nearby bathroom, so they could wash up, prepping like they were in a hospital rather than the basement of a suburban house.

Chapter 13

When they stepped into the bedroom, the sterile atmosphere was almost chilling. It looked too clean, too perfect for a place like this. Dr. Abagnale and Shelby made note of how close it felt to the private facilities they'd used before, almost impressed by Biggie's attention to detail. Shirvetta lay on the bed, now in the gown, her eyes fluttering with anticipation and anxiety.

"You ready?" Dr. Abagnale asked, looking her in the eyes.

Shirvetta nodded. "Yeah, let's do this."

Dr. Abagnale placed the mask over her face and the gas hissed softly as it went to work. Seconds later, her body went limp, her eyes closed, and the tension seemed to melt from her features.

"She's out?" Dr. Abagnale asked, glancing at Shelby.

She checked the monitors and gave him a thumbs-up. "Out."

"Good," he said, snapping on his gloves with a calm precision. "Let's begin."

The room fell into an eerie silence as the surgery began. The only sounds were the soft, clinical movements of instruments and the rhythmic beep of the heart monitor. Biggie and Baby Girl stood outside the room, waiting, their thoughts racing through everything else that was happening in their world. The surgery was just one piece of a puzzle that was spinning wildly out of control.

For now, though, all they could do was wait and pray that when it was over, their mother would be okay, and that this operation would be the least of the chaos they had to handle.

"The operation was a success," Dr. Abagnale announced, stepping out of the bedroom, with Shelby trailing behind.

Biggie's face broke into a wide grin. He grabbed Dr. Abagnale's hand, pulling him into a firm handshake and clapping him on the back. "Good lookin' out, Doc. Thank you," he said, gratitude dripping from every word.

"Thank you. Thank you," Baby Girl added, rushing over to hug Shelby with a sudden burst of emotion.

Shelby hesitated at first, caught off guard by the embrace, but smiled weakly and hugged her back, though it was clear she wasn't used to this level of warmth.

Dr. Abagnale cleared his throat, cutting through the moment. "Your mother should wake up in about an hour. Everything went as planned," he said, his voice steady and reassuring. He glanced toward the bathroom. "Shelby and I are gonna go wash up and get ourselves together."

Biggie nodded, his smile still wide. "Yeah, yeah, do your thing, Doc."

A few minutes later, the Abagnales returned, freshened up and ready to head out. Baby Girl handed Dr. Abagnale a knapsack, heavy with the weight of his payment. He felt the heft of it, smiling to himself, and gave Biggie another firm handshake.

"Man, I can't thank you enough," Biggie said, still holding the doctor's hand.

Dr. Abagnale chuckled, slipping the knapsack over his shoulder. "No problem. Always good doin' business with you."

Biggie's eyes twinkled with a mischievous glint. "You know, Doc, why don't you stay for a drink? We gotta celebrate, right?"

Shelby glanced at her husband, her discomfort clear. "I think we really should be going," she said, her voice edged with tension.

But Dr. Abagnale wasn't paying attention to his wife. His eyes had locked onto the bottle of Louis XIII sitting on a shelf behind the bar, a rare, expensive cognac he could never resist. He gave Shelby a quick look, dismissing her concerns. "One drink won't hurt, honey. We should toast a successful surgery, don't you think?"

Biggie smiled wide, throwing his arm around the doctor's shoulders. "That's what I'm talkin' about. Come on, Doc. Let's get you set up." He guided Dr. Abagnale to the bar, sliding a stool out for him to sit on.

"Come sit with me, Shelby," Baby Girl said, motioning to the empty stool beside her. "What you drinking?"

Shelby hesitated, then sighed. "I'll take an apple martini if you don't mind."

Biggie smirked. "I gotchu," he said, sliding Dr. Abagnale a glass of Louis XIII. "What about you, Doc? How's that?"

Dr. Abagnale took a deep sip, closing his eyes as he savored the rich flavor. "Man, this is top shelf. Real top shelf." He took another sip, clearly pleased.

The night rolled on, and that "one drink" turned into two, three, and six. Dr. Abagnale was a full-blown lush, leaning into the bar, talking too loudly and laughing too easily. On the other hand, Shelby was pacing herself, cutting herself off after her second martini. She'd been through this routine with her husband too many times. She knew how quickly he could spiral, and she wasn't about to get stuck cleaning up his mess.

Eventually, Shelby checked her watch and decided enough was enough. She stood up, gently pulling on her husband's arm. "Alright, that's it. We should go, darling."

Dr. Abagnale, now thoroughly drunk, waved her off, but eventually let her lead him toward the door. He grabbed the knapsack and gave one last, sloppy smile to Biggie and Baby Girl. "Take care, you two."

Shelby exchanged numbers with Baby Girl on their way out, talking about meeting up sometime soon. Once the door clicked shut behind them, the energy in the room shifted hard.

***

Chick pulled up three houses down from the armory where the twins and Shirvetta were holed up. She moved like the wind blew, her duster billowing behind her as she pulled her shotgun from under it and tucked it close to her side. She crouched low behind a row of bushes and scanned the house like a cat burglar.

The sound of locks being undone snapped her into action mode. Her brows furrowed as she saw a middle-aged man and woman, people who didn't belong. *Who the fuck is this?* Chick thought. But questions were for later. They were about to be caught up in some shit bigger than them. As the door creaked open, Chick's muscles coiled as she prepared to strike.

Before the woman could pull the door shut, Chick jacked the shotgun's pump with a quick and deliberate motion. The metallic click echoed in the silence like a cowbell, and she squeezed the trigger. The weapon jerked in her hands, spitting fire and smoke. The first shot caught the doctor in the chest and made him do a chaotic somersault. He landed face-first on the ground, with a knapsack of cash spilling beside him. His body twitched once, twice, and then went still.

The second blast hit his wife square in the chest, as she fumbled to close the door. She flew into the house and slid across the hardwood floor. Lying on her back, she stared up at the ceiling with wide, panicked eyes, gasping for air.

Chick stepped over the doctor's lifeless body and climbed up the porch steps. Entering the house, she walked up to the woman and nudged her with the barrel of the shotgun. She was still alive, barely. Her breaths came in shallow, ragged bursts, each one a struggle. Chick watched her a moment before leveling the shotgun at her face and pulling the trigger. The blast silenced the woman's struggling breaths instantly. Blood and shards of bone splattered against the walls as the woman's face disappeared.

Before Chick could make her next move, gunfire erupted from the basement door. The first shot hit her in the shoulder and spun her around. The second ripped through the leather of her duster and grazed her ribs. Snarling, Chick dropped to one knee and gritted her teeth against the pain. She pumped the shotgun, firing back without hesitation. Her shot snatched Biggie off his feet and sent him tumbling down the staircase. He hit the floor below with a hard thud.

Chick rushed to the basement door, face set in a grimace of pain and determination. She moved quickly but cautiously, her steps light on the staircase. Biggie had vanished, but his bloody trail gave him away.

"Lock the door. Lock the fuckin' door," Biggie's voice bellowed from deeper in the basement.

Chick followed the trail, her shotgun ready to finish the job. When she reached the bottom, Biggie popped out from behind the bar, firing shots wildly. Chick rolled across the floor and came up firing. Her blast shattered the bottles behind him, sending glass and booze raining down over the bar.

She crawled military-style behind the couch and pulled out a Zippo lighter. Flicking it open, she produced a flame and tossed it toward the bar. The alcohol ignited instantly and engulfed the space in roaring flames. Biggie's screams filled the room as he stumbled out from behind the bar, clothes, hair, and skin ignited in a bright, violent blaze.

His desperate attempt to raise his gun was met with the cold efficiency of Chick's shotgun. The blast struck him in the chest, lifting him off his feet and slamming him against the shelves of liquor. Bottles crashed down around him, and glass cut into his flesh as he crumpled to the floor.

Chick moved toward the bedroom door. She tried the knob, but it was locked. She kicked at it once, then twice, but the door refused to give. Frustrated, she raised her shotgun and blasted the lock off. The wood splintered and cracked, leaving a gaping hole where the lock had been.

Tossing the spent shotgun aside, she drew her Peacemaker revolver and cocked its hammer. She reached through the hole to unlock the door, but the moment her hand went through, gunshots rang out from the other side. Chick screamed as bullets ripped through her hand and forearm, the burning pain nearly unbearable. She yanked her hand back and examined the hole in her oozing palm.

Chick tried kicking the door again, but before her boot could connect, three more shots punched through the wood. The force knocked her off her feet and sent her sprawling to the floor.

Chick lay motionless and quiet, hearing Cowboy's voice inside her head.

Mommy, get up before they get away. Shirvetta has to pay. She took you away from pops. She took you away from me.

Those were the magic words. Chick's eyes pop open like she was resurrected from the dead. She grimaced as she got up from the floor, thankful she'd thought to wear a bulletproof vest. She tore a length of fabric from the lower half of her shirt and ripped it into halves. Using one to tie up her wounded hand, and the other to tie up the wound in her arm.

Holstering her revolver, Chick scanned the basement for something she could use to get through the bedroom door. Her eyes locked onto an emergency fire ax in a rectangle-shaped glass enclosure. Using her elbow, she cracked the enclosure until glass rained to the floor, and removed the ax. Looking at the ax, Chick knew it was perfect for the job. She approached the door, lifted the ax, and brought it down with all her might.

***

Biggie paced the floor, clenching his fists as he glared at Baby Girl. "We gotta get Golden," he growled. "We make 'em talk. We find Cowboy, we save Ma. Simple as that."

Baby Girl stood her ground, arms folded across her chest, eyes blazing with defiance. "We're not touching Golden, Biggie. He's our brother."

Biggie scoffed, stepping closer, looming over her. "So, what? We let Cowboy's crazy ass live so he can take out ma, whenever he gets good and ready? We lost pops already. I'm not losing ma for nobody. We ain't got time for your soft heart right now."

The room felt heavy as the tension crackled like a live wire between them. Baby Girl's jaws tightened. "We'll figure something else out. But I'm not touching either of our brothers," she said, her voice lower but unwavering. "You're not crossing that line. I'm not crossing that line. Not with family."

Biggie's eyes flashed with anger and his chest heaved. "What family, Baby Girl? The one that's tearin' itself apart 'cause of him?" He was so close now that she could feel the heat of his rage.

Then, without warning, Baby Girl slapped the shit out of him, her palm ringing out across the room. For a split second, the shock flickered in Biggie's eyes before the anger erupted like a storm. With a growl, he grabbed her by the shoulders and shoved her up against the wall, his face inches from hers, teeth bared.

"Don't chu ever put your hands on me again," he snarled, fists clenched so hard his knuckles bulged. "You hear me?"

Baby Girl stared him down, breathing heavily, but the fire in her eyes never faltered. "You gonna hit me, Biggie? Just like Cowboy hit Ma?" Her voice was sharp, cutting through the thick air between them.

Biggie froze, her words hitting him harder than any punch could. His grip loosened, and his shoulders slumped. He looked away, ashamed, the realization sinking in. He had sworn to never become like the men they hated, yet here he was, almost walking the same path.

"I'm sorry," he muttered, barely able to meet her eyes. "I didn't mean..."

But before he could finish, he heard the deafening roar of a shotgun from outside. Biggie's head snapped up, his brows furrowed in confusion. "What the hell?" he whispered, drawing his gun instinctively.

Baby Girl grabbed her pistol from her waistband and moved to the window, peeking through the curtains.

"Something's up," she said, voice tinged with unease.

Biggie nodded, all traces of their fight forgotten. He walked toward the door, pausing for a moment to glance back at her. "Stay here with Ma. I'll check it out."

Baby Girl swallowed as she felt her pulse quicken. "Be careful, Biggie," she said, disappearing through the bedroom door.

As Biggie stepped through the basement door, the tension in the air shifted and a new sense of danger loomed just beyond the walls.

Chapter 14

Baby Girl turned to Shirvetta, who was stirring weakly in bed.

"What's happenin', Baby?" Shirvetta asked, her voice a raspy whisper.

"I don't know, Ma, Biggie's checkin' it out," Baby Girl said.

For a few moments, there was only silence, the kind that made Baby Girl's skin crawl. Then, suddenly, the crackle of gunfire echoed from upstairs, followed by the sound of something, or someone, tumbling down the staircase.

Biggie's body hit the floor at the bottom of the stairs, hard. He groaned, pushing himself up, limping toward the bar as fast as his battered body would allow. His face was pale, sweat dripping from his brow. "Lock the door. Lock the fuckin' door," he ordered, his voice tight with pain.

Baby Girl sprang into action, locking the bedroom door and then dragging a heavy dresser against it, barricading them in. She grabbed her mother's coat, draping it over Shirvetta's frail shoulders before helping her into a chair in the corner. The air was thick with the smell of smoke and crackling of a fire somewhere in the basement.

Baby Girl heard Biggie screaming and firing his gun. Then the chaotic roars of a shotgun intervened. Tears burst through her eyes, but she quickly wiped them away. She didn't know if it was their connection as twins or what, but she knew without a doubt Biggie was dead.

"What's goin' on, Baby?" Shirvetta asked again, more desperate this time.

"I don't know, Ma. Just, just hang tight, okay?" Baby Girl's voice trembled as she gripped her gun tightly. Her heart pounded in her chest. Her every muscle was tense and ready for whatever came next.

Then, there it was, the sound that made her blood as cold as ice water. The bedroom door rattled violently, as if someone was trying to break it down. Kicks echoed through the room, powerful and relentless. Baby Girl's heart raced faster. Whoever was on the other side of that door was out for blood.

The lock suddenly blew out with a sharp crack, and for a moment, everything seemed to freeze. Baby Girl held her breath as her finger hovered over the trigger.

A face appeared in the doorway and peered through the splintered wood. Her stomach dropped as she recognized who it was.

"It's Cowboy," she gasped, fear tightening around her throat like a vice. "It's Cowboy."

Her mother's eyes widened in horror. "No," Shirvetta whispered.

Without hesitation, Baby Girl raised her gun and pulled the trigger twice. She heard Cowboy holler in pain as her bullets tore into his hand and possibly more. He fell back, cursing loudly, but it didn't stop him. The kicks came again, harder this time.

Baby Girl's heart raced as she emptied her gun into the door, hoping to keep him down, but the fire outside the room was spreading fast. Desperate, she rushed to the window, pushed it open, and turned to help her mother.

"We gotta go, Ma," she said breathlessly, trying to lift Shirvetta.

"But what about Biggie?"

"Biggie's dead, Ma."

Shirvetta's face contorted in grief and fresh tears spilled down her cheeks. "Not my lil' chunky man. Not my Biggie."

Baby Girl couldn't afford to cry. She couldn't afford to feel. She had to survive. They both did.

Behind her, the bedroom door splintered again, this time under the heavy blows of an ax.

The sound of the ax crashing into the door sent splinters flying across the room. Baby Girl's heart thumped as the fire outside the room crackled louder. She glanced back at the window and urged her mother to move faster.

"Come on, Ma. We gotta go, *now*," Baby Girl pleaded, her vocal cords heavy with fear.

Shirvetta nodded weakly and struggled to get her legs under her. Baby Girl helped her up and guided her toward the open window.

Crack.

Splinters exploded from the door frame as Chick's ax crashed into the barrier. Baby Girl's pulse quickened and her head snapped toward the sound. She saw Chick's silhouette in the wreckage of the door, the ax gleaming in the light of the fire.

Like a coyote closing in on a feral rabbit, Chick's eyes were wild. Her breath came in sharp, labored gasps, but there was no mistaking the fury burning behind her gaze. She pulled the ax back, kicked what was left of the door in, and stepped into the room with a vengeance.

Baby Girl's heart leaped into her throat. "Go, Ma, go," she urged, practically shoving Shirvetta toward the window.

"Come on, Mommy. They're getting away," Chick heard Cowboy's eerie calm voice in her head.

"Don't worry, Junior. Mommy's gon' get these bitchez, don't nobody fuck with my baby."

"Who the fuck is he talking to?" Baby Girl frowned, glancing back at Cowboy. She may have seen her oldest brother, but his dead mother had control of him.

Shirvetta was halfway out the window when Baby Girl gave her one last push. "Go, Ma. I'm right behind you," she yelled.

Once Shirvetta had cleared the window, Baby Girl threw her leg out of it, straddling the windowpane. Hearing hurried footsteps, she looked over her shoulder and Chick was charging at her, ax held above her head. As Chick brought the ax down, Baby Girl fell out of the window, missing the ax as it bit into the windowpane.

The fire from the other side of the door swept inside the room while Chick attempted to pull the ax out. Chick had trouble retrieving the ax so she climbed out the window and dropped to the asphalt below. Seeing Baby Girl and Shirvetta hopping into their car, she drew her revolver and went after them.

"They're getting away. We gotta catch them, Mommy," Cowboy's voice had a strange and unsettling urgency to it.

Baby Girl fired up her car and sped away. Chick fired at the back of the vehicle as it blew past her. Then she hopped in her whip and chased after her.

Baby Girl swung out into the street and Chick swung out behind her. Chick chased after Baby Girl's car on some action movie type of shit.

Chick focused on the road as she weaved in and out of lanes, nearly side-swiping cars and hitting pedestrians, trying not to lose Baby Girl. Baby Girl swerved from left to right, trying not to lose control of the car as she made a sharp turn at the corner. Shirvetta snatched the gun off her daughter's hip and hung out of the window, turning in Chick's direction and blasting. The windshield of Chick's vehicle broke up as it was struck by gunfire. Chick swerved trying to avoid the line of fire and almost collided with another car coming from the opposite direction. Shirvetta tried to keep firing, but the gun would no longer fire. So, she ducked back inside the car and examined it.

"What happened, Ma? Why'd you stop shooting at 'em?" Baby Girl asked, glancing at her mother.

"Goddamn gun jammed. Fuck," Shirvetta cursed, attempting to unjam the weapon. Right then, Chick sped up on the driver's side of Baby Girl's ride and pointed her stick at her.

Baby Girl's eyes widened in terror when she saw the barrel of the pistol Chick was aiming at her. Shirvetta was just as afraid when she saw it.

"Baby Girl, duck," she shouted, ducking low and pulling Baby Girl along. The driver's window exploded as bullets crashed through it and hit the passenger side of the windshield.

Baby Girl mashed the gas and widened the distance between her ride and Chick's. Hearing a driver lying on their horn, she looked up and saw a box truck coming her way. She'd unconsciously drifted into the lane of oncoming traffic. Baby Girl cut the wheel to the right and her car rose from its tires. She screamed as her car flipped, rolling over six times, sending debris flying in all directions before coming to a smoking halt. The vehicle burst into flames and the fire spread rapidly.

Shirvetta lay amidst broken glass grimacing as blood seeped from the gash in her forehead. She looked at Baby Girl, who was hanging upside down. She struggled to unbuckle her safety belt, but the mechanism wouldn't budge. Shirvetta crawled over to her and tried to unbuckle it herself, but she wasn't having luck either.

"It's stuck, ma. It's stuck," Baby Girl cried.

"Hold on, baby. I'ma come around to the other side," Shirvetta crawled out of the car and limped around to the driver's side. On her knees, she tried unbuckling the safety belt again, but it still wouldn't come free.

Baby Girl took note of how hot it had become as she started sweating. Her forehead creased with worry, fearing the car would explode any moment then.

"Ma," Baby Girl called for her mother's attention.

"Come on, you goddamn thang," Shirvetta cursed in frustration. She became so angry she started violently tugging on the safety belt.

"Ma," Baby Girl shouted harshly, snapping her mother out of it. Shirvetta looked at her like *What is it?* "It's over, Ma. You've gotta go, just go."

Shirvetta sobbed and shook her head. "I can't. I won't. You're my baby girl."

"Ma, please, listen to me, you've gotta go," Baby Girl's voice cracked emotionally, tears bursting from her eyes. "It doesn't make sense for us both to die."

Shirvetta made an ugly face as she cried, staring at her daughter. It was going to kill her to leave her there, but she was right. "I love you, baby," she whispered, kissing Baby Girl's forehead.

"I love you, too, Ma," Baby Girl said.

Shirvetta took one last look at her daughter before limping away as fast as she could. Baby Girl closed her eyes and recited a silent prayer. As she began crossing her heart, the car exploded, and flames shot into the sky.

Shirvetta sobbed harder as she limped down the road. She glanced over her shoulder and the headlights of Chick's car were closing in on her. The bright orbs shined at her back, making her look like a dark figure. Chick slid halfway out the driver-side window, pulling the trigger of her revolver.

Bullets smacked the ground near Shirvetta's dirty feet and debris went up in the air. The hot lead whizzed by her and nearly grazed her flesh. Her adrenaline surged through her body as her heart thumped crazily in her chest. She thought she was doing a decent job of dodging the gunfire, weaving back and forth in a frantic zig-zag. But little did she know, Chick was missing on purpose. She was only toying with her, corralling her like prey into a corner, her every move pushing her deeper into the trap.

Shirvetta's breath came in ragged gasps. Sweat rolled down her forehead and into her eyes, blurring her vision. She ran, her body shaking from fear and exertion, occasionally glancing over her shoulder at the soft-gray '85 Buick Regal following her like a bloodhound on the scent. It loomed behind her like a nightmare on wheels.

Shirvetta knew she was in her final moments, the countdown to her demise was ticking down with every second. Her only chance now, short of divine intervention, was to strike a deal with the Devil.

"Son, please, I'm sorry," she shouted over her shoulder, desperation tearing at her voice as she ran like a pack of wolves was breathing down her neck. Her lungs burned, and her legs felt like they were made of lead, but she kept going, fueled by sheer terror.

Suddenly, Shirvetta disappeared. It was as if the earth had swallowed her whole, but in reality, she had slipped over the edge of a cliff. Her scream resonated through the night as she tumbled down, sharp rocks tearing at her clothes and flesh. Each impact sent jolts of hot pain through her body until she finally landed with a harsh thud at the bottom.

The Buick Regal screeched to a halt at the edge of the cliff. Hopping out, Chick holstered her warm pistol and grabbed her flashlight. She twisted the end of it, flicking it on, the light sputtering weakly. A few hard smacks brought the beam to life and cast a narrow cone of light down into the ravine.

There she was, Shirvetta, lying at the bottom, her body broken, limbs twisted at impossible angles, her face bloody and contorted in agony. The beam of light cut harshly across her face, making her squint and turn away. But even in her pain, she could see the twisted smile that crept across Chick's lips. She had her where she wanted her. She could easily climb down to finish the job, but where was the fun in that? No, she decided to let whatever lurked in the darkness take care of her.

Chick walked back to her car and slammed the door shut. The engine roared to life, and she backed up, spinning her tires before tearing away from the cliffside. She cranked up the stereo, drowning out the faint, desperate cries that followed her into the night.

Shirvetta's breath was ragged, each exhale rattling in her chest as she strained her eyes, trying to pierce the darkness. The eerie noises grew closer, the rustle of leaves, the distant hoots of an owl. Her heart jumped at the sound, nearly stopping in her chest. Before she could even react, she felt tiny feet crawling across her and the sharp nips of rodents sinking into her flesh. Pain exploded across her body as they tore at her skin and drew blood. They gnawed and chewed, feasting on her like a swarm of ravenous locusts.

Then came the larger creatures, rats, raccoons, their claws digging into her as they joined the feast. Her screams cut through the darkness, rising in pitch and volume, creating a symphony of suffering that seemed to call out to the night. She felt every bite, every tear, as her flesh was ripped away. Her screams echoed through the empty woods, a horror movie come to life, until finally, her voice was silenced forever.

Chapter 15

Chick sat outside the precinct, the orange glow of her cigarette casting flickers of light across her face. The cold metal of the spurs on her boots clicked rhythmically against the curb as she tapped her foot, each sound a reminder of what was coming.

"And you're sure you wanna go through with this, Junior?" she asked, blowing out a cloud of smoke, her voice low and steady.

"Yeah, Mommy. I'm sho'," Cowboy's gruff voice replied in her head, as if he were sitting right there. "This is the only way I see myself being with Pops again."

Chick closed her eyes, taking a slow drag of her cigarette and blowing smoke. "Alright. I think this is crazy, but I know once yo' mind is made up, there's no changing it." She smirked slightly, shaking her head. "Just lemme finish this cancer stick."

She stared at the entrance of the precinct one last time before pushing herself off the curb and flicking the butt of her square aside.

This was it.

***

The heavy doors of the precinct swung inward as Chick strode inside, her metal spurs clinking like coins rattling in a tin can. Every step echoed, drawing curious eyes from cops, criminals, and civilians alike. Conversations halted and phones lowered. They stared, puzzled by the blood-stained duster that trailed behind her like a ghost.

She approached the front desk, where a grizzled officer was mid-conversation on the phone. His eyes landed on her and froze in disbelief. She looked like she'd walked straight out of a western nightmare.

"I've got some info on a few homicides," Chick announced coldly.

The officer blinked. "I'm sorry, ma'am, but you'll have to call back." The officer hung up the phone in haste.

***

Mommy, you know 9 is on the other side of that glass, right? Cowboy's voice echoed in Chick's mind. *I bet they're staring at us like some kinda zoo animal.*

Chick smirked to herself. "Yeah, I know, baby boy. Never mind them, though. They can think whatever they wanna think, long as we get what we came here for."

Cowboy's voice came again, proud and determined. *Alright, Mommy.*

Leaning back in her chair, Chick's spurs scraped the floor softly. "When this detective comes back, you lemme do all the talking. You've done yo' part, son. Now it's on me."

***

On the other side of the glass, two detectives watched her closely. One stood against the wall with his arms folded across his chest. The other sipped from a fresh cup of steaming hot coffee.

"You think this nutjob's gonna be found fit to stand trial?" the detective with his arms folded asked. "She's talking to herself."

131

The one with the coffee shrugged. "Who knows? Doesn't matter. As long as we can put one more of these animals behind bars, I'm good."

The other detective nodded. "Amen to that."

***

Back in the interrogation room...

Chick's ears perked up at the sound of footsteps approaching. She muttered under her breath, "Hush now, baby boy. Here he comes."

The detective who had been watching her from behind the glass walked in, pulled out a chair, and dropped into it. He laid a file on the table and then a pen. "Okay. Got authorization for the deal."

Chick's eyes narrowed as she looked over the document carefully, her free hand tracing the words before she signed it with a slow, deliberate stroke. She slid the ink pen and the document back toward the detective.

Alright, son, she thought to Cowboy. *It's signed now, we're on the fast track to being cellmates with your dad.*

The detective took the document and slid it into a folder, looking at her with a raised brow. "Anything else I can get you?"

Chick tilted her head, her smirk returning. "Yeah. Gemme a Newport."

The detective scoffed, shaking his head as he stood. "Sure. Why not?" He left the room, the heavy door clanging shut behind him.

Chick leaned back again and exhaled slowly. She could feel Cowboy's presence beside her. It was stronger now.

Mommy, we did it. We're going to be with Pop again.

"Yeah, baby boy," she whispered to the empty room. "We're gonna be together again. All three of us. Just like it shoulda been from the start."

The air in the room felt heavy, as if time itself was holding its breath. Chick sat quietly, staring at the mirror, knowing this was only the beginning of something much darker.

And there was no turning back.

***

When Heavy found out the twins had been murdered, he couldn't help feeling at fault, since he was the one who gave Cowboy the address where they and their mother were. When he caught wind Cowboy would be locked up in the same prison as him, he fashioned a knife to put through him for his disobedience but changed his mind once he thought about it. He reasoned, if it wasn't for him and Shirvetta teaching them the stickup game, then they wouldn't have adopted all the troubles they had, and probably wouldn't have been at each other's throats either. So, he was to be blamed. The way he saw it, he may as well have been on the scene pulling that trigger alongside Cowboy. Heavy decided to rebuild his relationship with Cowboy once he touched the yard, instead. They'd been apart for quite some time and had a lot of catching up and healing to do. Heavy was surprised when Quentin started gathering his things to move out, telling him he was getting a new cellmate. Heavy thought it may have been Cowboy who'd be his new bunkie, but then again that would be crazy to have another one of his sons sharing the same prison and cell as him.

***

A corrections officer led Cowboy through a labyrinth of gray corridors, past rows of cells where hardened men stood at the bars, sizing him up. Cowboy's steps echoed through the halls and his heart pounded harder with each step.

He wasn't just here as any other inmate, he was here to face Heavy, his father. The man who had taught him the

133

game, raised him in the streets, and who he hadn't seen in what felt like a lifetime. The man who might be planning to put a knife through his ribs the second they crossed paths for what he'd done. The weight of that reality pressed against Cowboy like an invisible hand around his throat.

When they reached the cell block, Cowboy's escort stopped in front of a barred door and unlocked it with a series of loud clanks. Stepping inside, Cowboy's body tensed as he scanned the narrow space. His stomach twisted. There, on the bottom bunk, sitting with his head bowed and hands clasped, was his dear old dad, Heavy.

The years in prison had added weight to Heavy's frame. His arms were thick and lined with veins and his skin was rough like an old, worn baseball mitt. His face was harder now and the gray strands in his goatee seemed to carry the weight of a thousand regrets.

Heavy's dark eyes locked onto Cowboy's, and for a moment, neither of them moved. The air between them buzzed with unspoken words and years of unresolved tension and broken trust. Cowboy swallowed and his nerves, choked the words he'd rehearsed on the bus ride over. He'd imagined this reunion so many times, but now, standing in front of his father, he felt like the scared little boy he'd once been, always desperate for Heavy's approval but never quite measuring up.

"Look who decided to pay his old man a visit." Heavy smiled.

Cowboy forced a smile. "Ain't like I had much of a choice, Pop."

Heavy stood up slowly and faced his firstborn. There was a long silence between them, then suddenly, Heavy pulled him into a hug. It wasn't the warm embrace of a father and son reuniting, but something stiff, awkward, a forced attempt at normalcy in their moment.

"Good to see you, Junior," Heavy muttered, patting Cowboy's back before taking a step back. He looked

Cowboy over like he was sizing him up, measuring the weight of the man standing before him.

"I didn't know if we'd ever see each other again," Cowboy told him.

"Shit. Neither did I." Heavy's tone was cool, but there was something beneath it, a vulnerability Cowboy had never seen before.

Once their awkward greeting was out of the way, Heavy made Cowboy aware of the prison politics and introduced him to the fellas in their area. After a while, things between them became like they were before Heavy was sent to prison. Cowboy thought it was a dream. Considering their circumstances, they were getting along beautifully. Although Heavy wanted to ask Cowboy about what went wrong that night that led him to kill the twins, he thought it was best to leave it alone, to not ruin their new beginnings.

One night, Heavy prepared to take a shower. Cowboy was going to join him, but stayed back because he had an important phone call he had to make. Heavy got undressed and stepped into his shower shoes. Entering the shower, he was surprised to see Quentin. He gave him a nod of acknowledgment and started lathering. Then he turned his back to the wall and began shampooing his hair. He had started washing the shampoo from his scalp when he felt a burning sensation pierce his torso.

Heavy's eyes popped open and he touched his wound. His fingers came away bloody. Quentin, eyes filled with rage, stood before him, naked as a newborn baby, with a gleaming shank in his fist.

Heavy wore a look of hurt and confusion. He didn't know what the fuck was up. The next thing he knew, Quentin charged at him again. He swung his shank, but Heavy managed to grasp his wrist with both hands. Quentin grasped his weapon with his other hand, lying all his weight against it. The strain showed on their faces and veins appeared on their necks.

"What is this about?" Heavy asked through clenched teeth.

"You wanna know what this is about? I'll tell you what the fuck this is about," Quentin said through clenched teeth.

***

Rolo assigned his younger cousin, Quentin, to house-sit and take care of his dogs while he was on "Baecation" with his girlfriend. Quentin was all for it since he'd have a frig full of food and all the weed he could smoke for the next three days. He got the surprise of a lifetime when he'd gone to take a shit, and overheard niggaz breaking in the spot.Quentin's back was pressed against the cold porcelain of the bathtub. Sweat dripped down his forehead and stung his eyes, but he didn't dare blink. Every muscle in his body was wound tight. His finger rested on the trigger of his gun, while he aimed it at the bathroom door. Through the thin walls, he could hear Heavy muttering as he worked the safe.

There were four of them, each one armed, trigger fingers itching, and ready to kill. Quentin's chest felt like a drumbeat against his ribs, his heart threatening to give him away. If just one of those Crimeys decided to take a leak or got curious, he was dead. He could hear the scrape of metal, a grunt of effort, and then the satisfying click of the safe door opening. Heavy's gravelly laugh cut through the silence like a blade.

"Got it," Heavy said with smug satisfaction.

Quentin's stomach twisted into knots. Every instinct screamed at him to jump out and shoot, but he wasn't suicidal. Not yet. The front door slammed shut, and their footsteps echoed down the hallway. He waited, forcing himself to count to thirty before he dared to move. His hand trembled slightly as he reached for the bathroom door, pushing it open inch by inch, the rusty hinges squeaking in protest.

He slid out into the hallway, gun first, his senses heightened, every nerve on edge. The room was empty, the shadows long and menacing in the moonlight filtering through the blinds. The safe stood open like a gaping wound, its contents gone. Quentin approached it slowly, his gaze darting around, half-expecting one of them to jump out and blast him. But they were gone. They'd taken everything.

"Shit," he cursed under his breath, slamming the side of his fist against the wall. Pain shot through his knuckles, but he barely felt it. He leaned back, knocking his head against the wall with a dull thud, feeling the weight of his failure settle in his gut like a stone. One job. Just one damn job, and he'd blown it. He could almost hear the thieves' laughter echoing in his mind, mocking him, taunting him.

Quentin took a deep breath, trying to steady himself and think. He needed a plan, something to fix this mess before it swallowed him whole. He could call Rolo, and try to spin this, but he wasn't a man you could bullshit. Quentin knew that much. If Rolo found out he'd been hiding like a scared bitch, while niggaz robbed him blind, he'd kill him. Quentin felt a cold sweat break out on his back. There was no room for cowards in Rolo's world.

Suddenly, Quentin's phone rang, its sound slicing through the heavy silence like a meat cleaver. His hands trembled as he stared at the unknown number flashing across the screen. For a moment, he hesitated and then answered.

"Yeah?" His voice was tight and strained.

"Quentin, baby," the voice on the other end was raw, broken, Rolo's mom. The words hit him like a slap. "I don't know how to tell you this, Rolo's gone. They... they killed him. It was a burglary, a home invasion gone wrong."

Quentin felt his blood run cold. "No, no, that can't be right," he mumbled, his voice barely a whisper.

"They shot him, Quentin. He didn't make it." Her voice cracked on the last word, and the sound of her sobs came through the line like a ghost haunting the air.

Chapter 16

Quentin stood frozen, the phone slipping from his ear. The words hung there, like shards of glass cutting into his brain. His cousin, Rolo, the only person who ever looked out for him, who had tried to warn him again and again that the streets were no place for a kid like him. Rolo was gone. Murdered.

Quentin's hands balled into fists, his knuckles turning white as memories of his big cousin flooded back. All the times Rolo had sat him down, looked him in the eye, and told him straight: *This life ain't for you, kid. You think you know, but chu don't. You gotta choice, Quent. Don't let this life choose for you.*

He hadn't listened. He thought he knew better. Thought he could handle the streets, and be a part of the game. Only now, he saw it wasn't a game, it was war, and war didn't care who it buried.

Quentin's grief twisted into something harder, sharper. A flame sparked in his gut, turning his sorrow into rage. He decided right then, in that moment of blinding clarity, that he would prove he was cut from the same cloth as Rolo. He would avenge his cousin's death, no matter what it took.

He began his hunt, scouring the streets for any whisper of the Crimeys, the crew who had made their name by being ruthless, by taking whatever they wanted. He tore through their world like a man possessed, following every lead, every rumor, every trail of blood they left behind.

One by one, he marked them off his list. Someone had laid the murder game down on them all, except Heavy, the last man standing.

That's when he heard about Butta, a loud-mouthed cousin of one of the Crimeys who got diarrhea by the mouth when he was drunk. Butta was known for hanging out at a dingy dive bar on the east side, a place where the floor stuck to your shoes, and the jukebox only played old blues records.

Quentin found him there on a Thursday night, sitting at the bar with a shot glass in one hand and a beer in the other. Butta was a big, thick-necked nigga with cowlicks, a patchy beard, and bloodshot eyes from a few too many drinks. He wore a leather coat that barely fit over his beer belly and had an obnoxious laugh that filled the foggy air with an annoying cackle.

Quentin, hood pulled low over his face, watched him from a dark corner of the bar. He went to use the men's room, but it must have been crowded. Because as soon as he walked in, he was walking back out. Butta stumbled out to the alley to take a piss, ignorant of the threat following him.

The outside air was the kind of cold that bit at your skin. Butta was leaning against the wall, muttering only God knew what as he unzipped his pants. Quentin moved quickly, slipping out of the shadows with cold, focused eyes.

"Hell you want?" Butta slurred and belched, breath stinking of cheap liquor.

Quentin was silent as he produced a tire iron from underneath his hoodie. It was heavy, shiny, and fit perfectly in his hand. He twirled it once, testing its weight, feeling the cold steel against his palm.

Butta squinted and tried to focus. Once his brain registered what was in Quentin's hands, he brandished a switchblade, but before he could make a move, Quentin pounced on him, swinging the tire iron with all the might he could muster.

The first blow landed against Butta's kneecap with a sickening crack. Butta screamed as his leg buckled beneath him and he crumpled to the ground.

"What the fuck, man," Butta yelled, clutching his leg, his voice high-pitched and panicked. "What chu want?"

Quentin's face was stone. "You know why I'm here, nigga."

Butta's eyes widened with realization, and panic set in. "Yo, I don't know what chu talking about. I don't—"

Another swing, this time to the ribs. The air whooshed out of Butta's lungs, and he doubled over, gasping for breath. Quentin grabbed him by his collar and looked him in the eyes.

"Tell me about Heavy," Quentin hissed, his voice low and threatening. "Tell me where he is."

Butta sputtered, blood trickling from the corner of his mouth. "I... I don't know, bruh. I swear to God, I don't—"

Quentin didn't wait. He brought the tire iron down again, smashing it against Butta's shoulder. The sound of bone crunching echoed off the brick walls. Butta screamed, his body jerking in pain.

"Last chance," Quentin said, his voice calm but edged with menace this time. "Where's Heavy?"

Butta whimpered, tears streaming down his face. "Alright, alright, yo. Son locked up, upstate. Doing big numbers."

"Where upstate? And if you bullshit me, I'ma crack yo' head like a rotten pumpkin. Speak." Quentin shook him by the collar violently.

Once Butta told him what he wanted to know, Quentin let him go and tossed the tire iron aside. As Butta bawled on the wet pavement, Quentin pulled out his cellphone and dialed 9-1-1, reporting what he'd done. Butta looked at him like he was insane, watching him walk back inside the bar.

Quentin ordered a couple of shots as he waited for the law. He had a nice little buzz going when the police finally arrived and arrested him.

Locked up on the island, he got confirmation of where Heavy was doing time.

Quentin stood tall during his trial. Every appearance his face stoic and his eyes were dark with purpose. An acquaintance of Rolo's, an old friend with deep pockets and deeper connections, paid off the judge in his case to make sure he landed in the same prison as Heavy. The gavel came down, and Quentin was sentenced, seven years for aggravated assault.

They would send him to Heavy, and once inside, he would do what he came to do.

***

As Quentin finished giving him the rundown, Heavy kneed him in his abdomen and punched him in the jaw. Quentin staggered back and caught himself before he could fall. Angrier than before, he rushed Heavy, swinging his bloodthirsty shank. Heavy ducked, twisted, and jumped back, narrowly avoiding the gleaming metal. Quentin lunged forward again, but Heavy was quicker. He caught Quentin's wrist and twisted it violently until a howl of pain erupted from Quentin's throat. Desperate, Quentin launched his other fist toward Heavy's jaw, but Heavy snatched it out of the air.

Heavy's face was a mask of rage as he slammed his forehead into Quentin's nose, breaking it. Quentin staggered back as blood gushed from his nostrils. But Heavy wasn't done with him yet. He rammed his knee into Quentin's gut, knocking the air from his lungs, and causing him to drop his shank with a clatter. Heavy took advantage and flipped Quentin over his shoulder. He crashed to the wet floor with a bone-jarring thud.

Heavy raised his foot to stomp Quentin's head, aiming to crush his skull, but Quentin rolled away just in time. Quentin struck out, punching Heavy's balls. Pain shot through Heavy like a glowing hot knife, and he doubled over, a guttural howl ripping from his throat. Quentin slammed his shin into Heavy's forehead and sent him crashing against the slick shower wall. Heavy's vision swam, and his breath came in ragged gasps. As his senses cleared, he saw Quentin charging again, shank in hand, its blade gleaming with menace.

Heavy barely managed to catch Quentin's wrist before the blade could pierce his pectoral muscle. They grappled, their bodies thrashing in a savage dance of death until they both hit the floor. Quentin, now straddling Heavy, pushed the shank toward his eye. Heavy's muscles strained and he turned his head, trying to avoid the blade's deadly point. The punch to his sack had weakened him. He felt his strength slipping away like sand between his fingers. Quentin's eyes danced wildly with blood lust. Clenching his jaws, he pressed down harder and the tip of the shank nearly pierced Heavy's eyeball.

Panic and a fierce determination surged through Heavy's veins. He shifted his weight, driving his knee up sharply into Quentin's balls. Quentin's face contorted in agony and his eyes bubbled. His grip on the shank loosened just enough for Heavy to slam his forehead into Quentin's broken nose again. Blood erupted in a crimson fountain, and Quentin's grip loosened further. Heavy swung his fist into Quentin's throat. Quentin choked, falling back and clawing at his neck.

Heavy lay back, his chest heaving, sucking in precious air. But Quentin was relentless. Through blood and fury, he snatched up the shank again, coming at Heavy like a raving lunatic. Just as the blade descended, a shadow emerged behind Quentin, Cowboy.

Cowboy, wearing a wicked grin, appeared like a mirage, and slammed his shank deep into Quentin's lung, twisting it with obsessive intensity. Quentin's eyes widened in shock and confusion. Blood bubbled from his lips and the shank slipped from his hand. Grinning maniacally, Cowboy pulled his blade across Quentin's abdomen, ripping through skin and muscle, letting Quentin's intestines spill like snakes onto the floor. Then, with cold, methodical cruelty, Cowboy stabbed the blade into Quentin's neck, slicing deep and wide. Blood sprayed across the shower walls, coating Heavy's face in a hot, crimson mist. Quentin collapsed to his knees, then face-first onto the floor, blood pooling and swirling down the drain.

Heavy, still gasping, allowed a weak smile. "Junior, I'm so glad to see y—"

His words died in his throat as his eyes widened in disbelief. He looked down to see Cowboy's shank buried in his stomach to its hilt. Cowboy twisted the blade slowly, savoring the moment, his other hand tenderly caressing Heavy's cheek.

"That's from mommy and me," Cowboy whispered, his voice eerily soft, almost sweet. He spoke as if he'd given him a gift.

Heavy's face twisted in shock and pain as Cowboy's gaze locked onto his. He had a crazed, almost loving stare. "Junior, what the—?"

Cowboy didn't let him finish. He stabbed him again, and again, each thrust harder than the last, driving the blade deeper into Heavy's flesh. Heavy's eyes clouded, blood bubbling at his lips, but Cowboy didn't let up. He kept stabbing, each strike more brutal than the last, a deranged grin stretching across his face.

Finally, Cowboy shoved his father off the blade. Heavy staggered back, his hands clenching his minced stomach, blood pouring between his fingers. He stumbled, his legs betrayed him, and collapsed against the shower wall, sliding down slowly. Heavy's eyes rolled to their corners and his body twitched as life abandoned him.

Cowboy looked up and smiled, eyes bright with an eerie calm. "I'm coming, mommy," he said to the ceiling. "I'm on my way to be with chu forever." With that, he dragged his blade from one side of his neck to the other, slitting his throat.

Blood sprayed and painted the shower walls in a nightmarish shade of red. Cowboy dropped the shank and collapsed to his knees, his breath gurgling. As his vision started to fade, a memory washed over him, his mother, pushing him on a swing at the park when he was just four years old. Tears rolled down his cheeks as his lips curled into a child's innocent smile.

"Faster, Mommy, faster," he heard his young voice scream in delight.

"You having fun, baby boy?" his mother's voice came warm and loving, a sound from a distant, happier time.

"Yeah," he whispered through his dying breaths. "This is the best day of my life."

"For real?"

"Unh huh. What was the best day of your life?" he asked.

"When you were born," she replied with the sweetest voice he'd ever heard.

Cowboy shut his eyes, his face relaxed into a peaceful smile, and his last breath escaped him. In his mind, he was back at the park, forever lost in that perfect, sunlit moment, his mother's laughter echoing in his ears as everything went black.

Epilogue

Poor Reese never made it out of the hood. It wasn't for lack of trying, but the streets had a way of pulling you back in. His little brothers, too young to know better, had taken some of the bread Chick had given him to school to flex. It was innocent, really, a bit of paper folded and waved around in the lunchroom, a way to feel big in a world that made you feel small. But word got back fast in the hood and it reached the wrong ears, a couple of stickup kids, hungry for a score, always on the lookout for just the right lick to get back on their feet.

The duo tracked the boys, watching them on their walk home, trailing them through the maze of cracked sidewalks, broken glass, gang bangers, and baseheads. They hung back just enough, shadows in the late afternoon sun, until the boys disappeared into their building. They waited, counted floors, and made a note of the apartment number. The plan was simple, just like it always was, go in quick, get the money, and get out. But plans never stayed simple in the projects.

They kicked the door in with a loud bang that echoed through the building, shaking the thin walls. Guns were drawn, and threats hurled.

"Give us the money or we wetting this bitch up," one of them yelled, voice steady, eyes red and threatening.

Reese's heart was pounding, but he wasn't built to be a victim, never had been. He reached for the piece he kept tucked in the waistband of his jeans, and before he knew it, an exchange of gunfire erupted, bullets flying in every direction like an old western shootout.

When the smoke cleared, the living room was a mess of overturned furniture, shattered glass, and blood. Reese looked down and saw one of his little brothers lying motionless, eyes wide open, staring at the ceiling as if searching for stars that had never been there. His chest felt like it had been ripped open. He turned and saw one of the stickup kids stretched out on the floor, face down in a pool of blood, his hand still gripping a gun. But the other one, the one who had taken the money, he was gone, vanished into the stairwell like a ghost.

That last bullet cost Reese more than money. It took a piece of his soul. His mother, already teetering on the edge of sanity, crumbled at the news. She screamed, and wailed, her voice a haunting cry that echoed through the block until one day she just broke. A nervous breakdown, they said, and before Reese knew it, they had her locked up in some asylum where the walls were padded and the windows had bars.

Then child protective services came knocking, poking around with their cold, pitying eyes, asking questions they had no right to ask. Reese felt the panic rise in his chest, the walls closing in on him. He couldn't let them take him, too. So, he did the only thing he could think of, he ran. He fled the projects with nothing but the clothes on his back, watching from a nearby rooftop as his remaining siblings were loaded into a big white van, like cattle, and whisked away to God knows where.

The streets became his home, but not like before. This time, he wasn't about that slow money, bagging up dope, playing lookout, hustling for scraps. That was kid's play. Reese had seen enough death to know there were quicker ways to get paid. He turned to a new trade, jacking. And he didn't just hit the streets, he embodied them.

They said it was crazy, the way he started dressing like Cowboy, wearing the same wide-brimmed hat and the same long duster that seemed to flow behind him like a curtain against a breeze. The little nigga was even packing the same twin Peacemaker revolvers as Cowboy. The streets whispered that it was like Cowboy's spirit had left his body when he died and found a new home in Reese's. Reese not only moved differently now, but he talked differently, too. He had a low, cold voice that sent chills through the block like an icy winter. He walked around like a man who didn't have shit to lose, but that was because he didn't.

The change in him was evident to anyone who had known him before. The light in his eyes had dimmed and was replaced by something harder. Something that glinted like shards of glass below a street lamp. The boy didn't flinch anymore, and he for damn sure didn't hesitate. There wasn't any fear in him, just a burning desire to take back what had been ripped from him, his family, his childhood, his future. And he wasn't stopping until he did.

Cowboy might have died in the shower that day, but his spirit lived on in Reese. The hood had claimed another soul, but this one was fighting back, and God help anyone who stood in his way.

Reese sat at the table inside his kitchen, cleaning his identical pistols and listening to a news report about two dopeboys found slumped dead inside a trap house. This was his work. Once he deemed his weapons cleaned, he picked one up, spinning its chamber and pointing its lethal end at the television's screen. Closing one eye, he aimed his revolver's barrel between the eyes of the news anchor and pulled its trigger. The weapon clicked as its hammer slammed against the firing pin.

Satisfied with the pistol's performance, he began loading bullets inside their cylinders. Once he was done, he shoved them inside their holsters and got ready for the day. First came the bulletproof vest, the duster, and finally the same wide-brimmed hat Chick had given him. He dropped to his knees at a shrine he'd made up for a Black Jesus Christ, surrounded by crosses, candles, prayer-beaded necklaces, and anything else one considered holy.

"Reese, I'm hungry," a small voice came from behind him.

Reese turned around to find his 7-year-old little brother, stretching his arms and yawning, having just gotten up. He had crust in the corners of his eyes and dry drool around his mouth.

"Make you some cereal or something until I get back. I'm already late for work," Reese replied, stealing a glance at his watch.

The dopeboys were already on the block tending to their morning rush of dope fiends. He knew he should have been on their heads an hour ago, running down on them for that dirty money.

"Okay," the boy ran inside the kitchen, placing a chair against the counter so he could reach the many boxes of cereal perched on top of the frig. He didn't want a traditional breakfast anyway. The cereal was right up his alley.

By the time Reese had concealed his Draco inside his coat, his little brother was sitting Indian style in front of the living room's television watching cartoons and munching on Froot Loops.

"A'ight, yo, I'm outta here," Reese ruffled his brother's head and kissed it. The door clicked shut behind him, leaving the child to his own devices.

***

Golden had been tested by life in ways that broke most men. Burying his entire family pushed him to the brink of madness, his mind spiraling into a darkness so deep he could feel the walls closing in. Alone in his crib, with a pistol shoved inside his grill, he prepared to pull the trigger.

But a higher power had intervened. The television on the wall before his bed, which had been playing static for hours, suddenly came to life with a late-night Christian program on BET. The voice of Minister Johnny K. Polight, an ex-pimp turned servant of God, echoed through the room with a conviction that broke through Golden's despair. He didn't know if it was the words themselves or the man's raw, unapologetic delivery, but something clicked inside him. He took the pistol from his mouth and gave Minister Polight his undivided attention.

From that night forward, Golden attended Minister Polight's church regularly. He became a fixture in the front pew, absorbing every word like a man starved for hope. A friendship blossomed between the two men, a bond that grew into a father-son relationship that Golden had longed for since the death of his father. With time, he became close to Polight's family and started dating his daughter, Christiana. A year later, they married, a glorious union celebrated with joy. They were now expecting their first child, a boy they decided to name Trust N Love, a name filled with the faith that had saved him from his darkest hour.

Golden and Christiana had just left the doctor's office, excited about the first ultrasound of their unborn child.

As they drove, Christiana's cravings took over. "Oxtails and rice, plantains, and some Neapolitan ice cream," she announced, grinning.

Golden smirked, pulling into a food spot and making his rounds, returning to the car with everything she wanted. He handed her the pint of ice cream, and she didn't waste any time digging in with a plastic spoon.

Golden glanced at her, wearing a smile on his face. "Now that's some real big back activity right there," he teased.

Christiana, her mouth full of ice cream, rolled her eyes. "Shut up," she mumbled through a grin.

"Gemme some," he pleaded, his eyes on the dessert.

She laughed. "How you gon' call me a big back and then ask for some of my ice cream?"

"Easy, big back, now gemme some," he said, leaning in closer. "The Lord said it's better to give than receive."

With a chuckle, she relented, feeding him a spoonful. The sweet ice cream hit his tongue, and he nodded in approval, already talking about doubling back to buy himself a pint.

As they pulled into a gas station, Christiana teased, "Trifling, not even gon' gemme a kiss."

Golden gave her three quick pecks before hopping out, glancing at the pump's number as he jogged to the attendant's window.

Inside the car, Christiana continued to savor her ice cream, but then her smile faded. A peculiar sound caught her attention, the unmistakable spinning and clicking of a revolver's chamber. Her brow furrowed as she glanced around, trying to locate the source, but she saw nothing. The sound grew louder, more menacing, like an omen on the wind. Bystanders began to look around, fear flickering in their eyes before they took off running.

A chill ran down Christiana's spine. Her spoon hovered in mid-air and her heartbeat quickened. She heard it again, louder this time, the clicking and spinning growing almost deafening.

***

"Gemme $80 on pump three and a pack of pink Starburst," Golden said, sliding a crisp hundred-dollar bill into the money tray. He paused, catching his reflection in the bulletproof glass. His shoulder-length locs framed his face and he had a smooth goatee, adding a mature edge to his appearance. He looked every bit the man he'd become, a man reborn and proud.

The attendant gave him his change and candy, but Golden's attention was elsewhere. He noticed people scattering, their hurried movements mirrored in the glass. A frown creased his brow as he heard it, the spinning and clicking of a revolver's chamber. His eyes darted around, searching for the source, but he did not see anything or anyone. The growing panic of the crowd triggered an alarm in his head. Something was wrong, very wrong.

Instinct screamed at him to run, and he sprinted back toward the car, abandoning his change. But in his haste, he stumbled and hit the ground hard. He winced, pain shooting up his arm as he looked up and saw it, a shadowy figure. His face was obscured beneath a wide-brimmed hat and a long duster coat. The man seemed to have materialized from nowhere, like a ghost with a purpose, walking toward Christiana.

Golden scrambled to his feet and instinctively reached for the gun he kept in his waistband. It wasn't there. Damn. He had stopped carrying a gun once he left the streets behind. Now, he needed one more than ever.

"Gemme all that shit, hurry up," the man barked, his Peacemaker revolver leveled at Christiana. She fumbled to hand over her purse and her hands trembled as she removed her diamond earrings.

Golden didn't think. He moved. Launching himself off the hood of his car, he tackled the man with all his weight and they hit the ground hard. They rolled back and forth on the ground, fighting for control of the gun, causing it to discharge twice. The first bullet whizzed past Golden's ear, but the second came so close, he could feel the heat near his head.

Christiana's eyes widened in terror as she watched her husband grapple with the armed man. She searched for something, anything, to help. Then it hit her, the tire iron in the trunk. She darted to the back of the car, her fingers fumbling with the latch before yanking it open. She grabbed the tire iron and turned to help.

But before she could reach them, a third gunshot rang out. She froze. Her breath caught in her throat as she saw the man in the duster stagger back. Golden's face was twisted in pain, a grimace that told her everything she feared. She dropped the tire iron, her hands trembling, her eyes locked on her husband.

"Just hadda be a hero," the man shook his head and picked up Christiana's purse. He kicked Golden viciously in the side and walked away, holstering his pistol. The way he strode one would have thought he'd just taken out the trash, instead of clapping someone.

Christiana fell to her knees, tears streaming down her face, her voice breaking into desperate sobs. "No, no, no. Golden!" She crawled to him, cradling his head in her lap, her hands shaking as she stroked his face. "It's gonna be okay, baby. Just hold on. Fight. You've gotta fight." Her voice wavered, panic clawing at her throat. "Help us. Somebody, help us," she screamed into the void, as distant sirens wailed, growing louder but feeling impossibly far away.

Around the corner, not far up the block, Reese strolled past the passenger window of a late-model Cadillac. In the glass, there was a reflection that wasn't his own, it was Cowboy's.

THE END

My Self-Published Books

BLOODY KNUCKLES 1-2
THE DEVIL WEARS TIMBS 1-7
ME AND MY HITTAZ 1-6
THE LAST REAL NIGGA ALIVE 1-3
A HOOD NIGGA'S BLUES
A SOUTH-CENTRAL LOVE AFFAIR
BURY ME A G 1-5
THE DOPEMAN'S BODYGUARD 1-2
FEAR MY GANGSTA 1-5
THESE SCANDALOUS STREETS 1-3
A GANGSTA'S EMPIRE 1-3
GOD BLESS THE TRAPPERS 1-3

Coming Soon

THEY MADE ME AN ANIMAL
THERE'S NO PLACE IN HEAVEN FOR THUGS

Lock Down Publications and Ca$h Presents
Assisted Publishing Packages

Due to an increase in the price of services we have increased our prices. The prices below reflect the price increase as of 11/1/24.

BASIC PACKAGE	UPGRADED PACKAGE
$699	**$1000**
Editing	Typing
Cover Design	Editing
Formatting	Cover Design
	Formatting
	Upload eBooks to Amazon
	Upload Paperback to Amazon
ADVANCE PACKAGE	**LDP SUPREME PACKAGE**
$1,400	**$1,700**
Typing	Typing
Editing (line editing/content)	Editing (line editing/content)
Cover Design	Cover Design
Formatting	Formatting
Copyright Registration	Copyright Registration
Proofreading	Proofreading
Upload eBooks to Amazon	Set up Amazon Account
Upload Paperback to Amazon	Upload eBooks to Amazon
	Upload Paperback to Amazon
	Advertise on LDP's Amazon and Facebook Page

***Other services available upon request.
Additional charges may apply

Lock Down Publications
P.O. Box 944
Stockbridge, GA 30281-9998
Phone: 470 303-9761
Email: lockdownpublications@gmail.com

Submission Guideline

Submit the first three chapters of your completed manuscript to ldpsubmissions@gmail.com. In the subject line add **Your Book's Title**. The manuscript must be in a Word Doc file and sent as an attachment. Document should be in Times New Roman, double spaced, and in size 12 font. Also, provide your synopsis and full contact information. If sending multiple submissions, they must each be in a separate email.

Have a story but no way to send it electronically? You can still submit to LDP/Ca$h Presents. Send in the first three chapters, written or typed, of your completed manuscript to:

LDP: Submissions Dept
P.O. Box 944
Stockbridge, GA 30281-9998

DO NOT send original manuscript. Must be a duplicate.
Provide your synopsis and a cover letter containing your full contact information.

Thanks for considering LDP and Ca$h Presents.

NEW RELEASES

BLOODLINE OF A SAVAGE 1&2
THESE VICIOUS STREETS 1&2
RELENTLESS GOON
RELENTLESS GOON 2
BY PRINCE A. TAUHID

THE BUTTERFLY MAFIA 1-3
BY FUMIYA PAYNE

A THUG'S STREET PRINCESS 1&2
BY MEESHA

CITY OF SMOKE 2
BY MOLOTTI

STEPPERS 1,2&3
THE REAL BADDIES OF CHI-RAQ
BY KING RIO

THE LANE 1&2
BY KEN-KEN SPENCE

THUG OF SPADES 1&2
LOVE IN THE TRENCHES 2
CORNER BOYS
BY COREY ROBINSON

TIL DEATH 3
BY ARYANNA

THE BIRTH OF A GANGSTER 4
BY DELMONT PLAYER

PRODUCT OF THE STREETS 1&2
BY DEMOND "MONEY" ANDERSON

NO TIME FOR ERROR
BY KEESE

MONEY HUNGRY DEMONS
BY TRANAY ADAMS

Coming Soon from Lock Down Publications/Ca$h Presents

IF YOU CROSS ME ONCE 6
ANGEL V
By Anthony Fields

IMMA DIE BOUT MINE 5
By Aryanna

A THUGS STREET PRINCESS 3
By Meesha

PRODUCT OF THE STREETS 3
By Demond Money Anderson

CORNER BOYS 2
By Corey Robinson

THE MURDER QUEENS 6&7
By Michael Gallon

CITY OF SMOKE 3
By Molotti

CONFESSIONS OF A DOPE BOY
By Nicholas Lock

THA TAKEOVER
By Keith Chandler

BETRAYAL OF A G 2
By Ray Vinci

CRIME BOSS
By Playa Ray

Available Now

RESTRAINING ORDER 1 & 2
By **CA$H & Coffee**

LOVE KNOWS NO BOUNDARIES 1-3
By **Coffee**

RAISED AS A GOON I, II, III & IV
BRED BY THE SLUMS I, II, III
BLAST FOR ME I & II
ROTTEN TO THE CORE I II III
A BRONX TALE I, II, III
DUFFLE BAG CARTEL I II III IV V VI
HEARTLESS GOON I II III IV V
A SAVAGE DOPEBOY I II
DRUG LORDS I II III
CUTTHROAT MAFIA I II
KING OF THE TRENCHES
By **Ghost**

LAY IT DOWN I & II
LAST OF A DYING BREED I II
BLOOD STAINS OF A SHOTTA I & II III
By **Jamaica**

LOYAL TO THE GAME I II III
LIFE OF SIN I, II III
By **TJ & Jelissa**

IF LOVING HIM IS WRONG…I & II
LOVE ME EVEN WHEN IT HURTS I II III
By **Jelissa**

PUSH IT TO THE LIMIT
By **Bre' Hayes**

BLOODY COMMAS I & II
SKI MASK CARTEL I, II & III
KING OF NEW YORK I II, III IV V
RISE TO POWER I II III
COKE KINGS I II III IV V
BORN HEARTLESS I II III IV
KING OF THE TRAP I II
By **T.J. Edwards**

WHEN THE STREETS CLAP BACK I & II III
THE HEART OF A SAVAGE I II III IV
MONEY MAFIA I II
LOYAL TO THE SOIL I II III
By **Jibril Williams**

A DISTINGUISHED THUG STOLE MY HEART I II & III
LOVE SHOULDN'T HURT I II III IV
RENEGADE BOYS 1-4
PAID IN KARMA 1-3
SAVAGE STORMS 1-3
AN UNFORESEEN LOVE 1-3
BABY, I'M WINTERTIME COLD 1-3
A THUG'S STREET PRINCESS 1&2
By **Meesha**

A GANGSTER'S CODE 1-3
A GANGSTER'S SYN 1-3
THE SAVAGE LIFE 1-3
CHAINED TO THE STREETS 1-3
BLOOD ON THE MONEY 1-3
A GANGSTA'S PAIN 1-3
BEAUTIFUL LIES AND UGLY TRUTHS
CHURCH IN THESE STREETS
By **J-Blunt**

CUM FOR ME 1-8
An LDP Erotica Collaboration

BLOOD OF A BOSS 1-5
SHADOWS OF THE GAME
TRAP BASTARD
By **Askari**

THE STREETS BLEED MURDER 1-3
THE HEART OF A GANGSTA 1-3
By **Jerry Jackson**

WHEN A GOOD GIRL GOES BAD
By **Adrienne**

THE COST OF LOYALTY 1-3
By **Kweli**

BRIDE OF A HUSTLA 1-3
THE FETTI GIRLS 1-3
CORRUPTED BY A GANGSTA 1-4
BLINDED BY HIS LOVE
THE PRICE YOU PAY FOR LOVE 1-3
DOPE GIRL MAGIC 1-3
By **Destiny Skai**

A KINGPIN'S AMBITION
A KINGPIN'S AMBITION II
I MURDER FOR THE DOUGH
By **Ambitious**

TRUE SAVAGE 1-7
DOPE BOY MAGIC 1-3
MIDNIGHT CARTEL 1-3
CITY OF KINGZ 1&2
NIGHTMARE ON SILENT AVE
THE PLUG OF LIL MEXICO 1&2
CLASSIC CITY
By **Chris Green**

A GANGSTER'S REVENGE 1-4
THE BOSS MAN'S DAUGHTERS 1-5
A SAVAGE LOVE 1&2
BAE BELONGS TO ME 1&2
A HUSTLER'S DECEIT 1-3
WHAT BAD BITCHES DO 1-3
SOUL OF A MONSTER 1-3
KILL ZONE
A DOPE BOY'S QUEEN 1-3
TIL DEATH 1-3
IMMA DIE BOUT MINE 1-4
By **Aryanna**

A DOPEBOY'S PRAYER
By **Eddie "Wolf" Lee**

THE KING CARTEL 1-3
By **Frank Gresham**

THESE NIGGAS AIN'T LOYAL 1-3
By **Nikki Tee**

GANGSTA SHYT 1-3
By **CATO**

THE ULTIMATE BETRAYAL
By **Phoenix**

BOSS'N UP 1-3
By **Royal Nicole**

I LOVE YOU TO DEATH
By **Destiny J**

I RIDE FOR MY HITTA
I STILL RIDE FOR MY HITTA
By **Misty Holt**

LOVE & CHASIN' PAPER
By **Qay Crockett**

TO DIE IN VAIN
SINS OF A HUSTLA
By **ASAD**

BROOKLYN HUSTLAZ
By **Boogsy Morina**

BROOKLYN ON LOCK 1 & 2
By **Sonovia**

GANGSTA CITY
By **Teddy Duke**

A DRUG KING AND HIS DIAMOND 1-3
A DOPEMAN'S RICHES
HER MAN, MINE'S TOO 1&2
CASH MONEY HO'S
THE WIFEY I USED TO BE 1&2
PRETTY GIRLS DO NASTY THINGS
By **Nicole Goosby**

LIPSTICK KILLAH 1-3
CRIME OF PASSION 1-3
FRIEND OR FOE 1-3
By **Mimi**

TRAPHOUSE KING 1-3
KINGPIN KILLAZ 1-3
STREET KINGS 1&2
PAID IN BLOOD 1&2
CARTEL KILLAZ 1-3
DOPE GODS 1&2
By **Hood Rich**

THE STREETS ARE CALLING
By **Duquie Wilson**

STEADY MOBBN' 1-3
THE STREETS STAINED MY SOUL 1-3
By **Marcellus Allen**

WHO SHOT YA 1-3
SON OF A DOPE FIEND 1-4
HEAVEN GOT A GHETTO 1&2
SKI MASK MONEY 1&2
By **Renta**

GORILLAZ IN THE BAY 1-4
TEARS OF A GANGSTA 1/&2
3X KRAZY 1&2
STRAIGHT BEAST MODE 1&2
By **DE'KARI**

TRIGGADALE 1-3
MURDA WAS THE CASE 1-3
By **Elijah R. Freeman**

SLAUGHTER GANG 1-3
RUTHLESS HEART 1-3
By **Willie Slaughter**

GOD BLESS THE TRAPPERS 1-3
THESE SCANDALOUS STREETS 1-3
FEAR MY GANGSTA 1-5
THESE STREETS DON'T LOVE NOBODY 1-2
BURY ME A G 1-5
A GANGSTA'S EMPIRE 1-4
THE DOPEMAN'S BODYGAURD 1&2
THE REALEST KILLAZ 1-3
THE LAST OF THE OGS 1-3
By **Tranay Adams**

MARRIED TO A BOSS 1-3
By **Destiny Skai & Chris Green**

KINGZ OF THE GAME 1-7
CRIME BOSS 1-3
By **Playa Ray**

FUK SHYT
By **Blakk Diamond**

DON'T F#CK WITH MY HEART 1&2
By **Linnea**

ADDICTED TO THE DRAMA 1-3
IN THE ARM OF HIS BOSS
By **Jamila**

LOYALTY AIN'T PROMISED 1&2
By **Keith Williams**

YAYO 1-4
A SHOOTER'S AMBITION 1&2
BRED IN THE GAME
By **S. Allen**

TRAP GOD 1-3
RICH $AVAGE 1-3
MONEY IN THE GRAVE 1-3
CARTEL MONEY
By **Martell Troublesome Bolden**

FOREVER GANGSTA 1&2
GLOCKS ON SATIN SHEETS 1&2
By **Adrian Dulan**

TOE TAGZ 1-4
LEVELS TO THIS SHYT 1&2
IT'S JUST ME AND YOU
By **Ah'Million**

KINGPIN DREAMS 1-3
RAN OFF ON DA PLUG
By **Paper Boi Rari**

THE STREETS MADE ME 1-3
By **Larry D. Wright**

CONFESSIONS OF A GANGSTA 1-4
CONFESSIONS OF A JACKBOY 1-3
CONFESSIONS OF A HITMAN
By **Nicholas Lock**

I'M NOTHING WITHOUT HIS LOVE
SINS OF A THUG
TO THE THUG I LOVED BEFORE
A GANGSTA SAVED XMAS
IN A HUSTLER I TRUST
By **Monet Dragun**

QUIET MONEY 1-3
THUG LIFE 1-3
EXTENDED CLIP 1&2
A GANGSTA'S PARADISE
By **Trai'Quan**

CAUGHT UP IN THE LIFE 1-3
THE STREETS NEVER LET GO 1-3
By **Robert Baptiste**

NEW TO THE GAME 1-3
MONEY, MURDER & MEMORIES 1-3
By **Malik D. Rice**

CREAM 2-3
THE STREETS WILL TALK
By **Yolanda Moore**

THE STREETS WILL NEVER CLOSE 1-3
By **K'ajji**

LIFE OF A SAVAGE 1-4
A GANGSTA'S QUR'AN 1-4
MURDA SEASON 1-3
GANGLAND CARTEL 1-3
CHI'RAQ GANGSTAS 1-4
KILLERS ON ELM STREET 1-3
JACK BOYZ N DA BRONX 1-3
A DOPEBOY'S DREAM 1-3
JACK BOYS VS DOPE BOYS 1-3
COKE GIRLZ
COKE BOYS
SOSA GANG 1&2
BRONX SAVAGES
BODYMORE KINGPINS
BLOOD OF A GOON
By **Romell Tukes**

CONCRETE KILLA 1-3
VICIOUS LOYALTY 1-3
By **Kingpen**

THE ULTIMATE SACRIFICE 1-6
KHADIFI
IF YOU CROSS ME ONCE 1-3
ANGEL 1-4
IN THE BLINK OF AN EYE
By **Anthony Fields**

THE LIFE OF A HOOD STAR
By **Ca$h & Rashia Wilson**

NIGHTMARES OF A HUSTLA 1-3
BLOOD AND GAMES 1&2
By **King Dream**

GHOST MOB
By **Stilloan Robinson**

HARD AND RUTHLESS 1&2
MOB TOWN 251
THE BILLIONAIRE BENTLEYS 1-3
REAL G'S MOVE IN SILENCE
By **Von Diesel**

MOB TIES 1-7
SOUL OF A HUSTLER, HEART OF A KILLER 1-3
GORILLAZ IN THE TRENCHES
By **SayNoMore**

BODYMORE MURDERLAND 1-3
THE BIRTH OF A GANGSTER 1-4
By **Delmont Player**

FOR THE LOVE OF A BOSS 1&2
By **C. D. Blue**

KILLA KOUNTY 1-5
By **Khufu**

MOBBED UP 1-4
THE BRICK MAN 1-5
THE COCAINE PRINCESS 1-10
STEPPERS 1-3
SUPER GREMLIN 1-4
By **King Rio**

MONEY GAME 1&2
By **Smoove Dolla**

A GANGSTA'S KARMA 1-4
By **FLAME**

KING OF THE TRENCHES 1-3
By **GHOST & TRANAY ADAMS**

QUEEN OF THE ZOO 1&2
By **Black Migo**

GRIMEY WAYS 1-3
BETRAYAL OF A G
By **Ray Vinci**

XMAS WITH AN ATL SHOOTER
By **Ca$h & Destiny Skai**

KING KILLA 1&2
By **Vincent "Vitto" Holloway**

BETRAYAL OF A THUG 1&2
By **Fre$h**

THE MURDER QUEENS 1-5
By **Michael Gallon**

FOR THE LOVE OF BLOOD 1-4
By **Jamel Mitchell**

HOOD CONSIGLIERE 1&2
NO TIME FOR ERROR
By **Keese**

PROTÉGÉ OF A LEGEND 1&2
LOVE IN THE TRENCHES 1&2
By **Corey Robinson**

THE PLUG'S RUTHLESS DAUGHTER
By **Tony Daniels**

BORN IN THE GRAVE 1-3
CRIME PAYS
By **Self Made Tay**

MOAN IN MY MOUTH
By **XTASY**

TORN BETWEEN A GANGSTER AND A GENTLEMAN
By **J-BLUNT & Miss Kim**

LOYALTY IS EVERYTHING 1-3
CITY OF SMOKE 1&2
By **Molotti**

HERE TODAY GONE TOMORROW 1&2
By **Fly Rock**

WOMEN LIE MEN LIE 1-4
FIFTY SHADES OF SNOW 1-3
STACK BEFORE YOU SPLURGE
GIRLS FALL LIKE DOMINOES
NAÏVE TO THE STREETS
By **ROY MILLIGAN**

PILLOW PRINCESS
By **S. Hawkins**

THE BUTTERFLY MAFIA 1-3
SALUTE MY SAVAGERY 1&2
By **Fumiya Payne**

THE LANE 1&2
By Ken-Ken Spence

THE PUSSY TRAP 1-5
By **Nene Capri**

DIRTY DNA
By **Blaque**

SANCTIFIED AND HORNY
by **XTASY**

BOOKS BY LDP'S CEO, CA$H

TRUST IN NO MAN
TRUST IN NO MAN 2
TRUST IN NO MAN 3
BONDED BY BLOOD
SHORTY GOT A THUG
THUGS CRY
THUGS CRY 2
THUGS CRY 3
TRUST NO BITCH
TRUST NO BITCH 2
TRUST NO BITCH 3
TIL MY CASKET DROPS
RESTRAINING ORDER
RESTRAINING ORDER 2
IN LOVE WITH A CONVICT
LIFE OF A HOOD STAR
XMAS WITH AN ATL SHOOTER